Awake in a New World
The New World Book One

Sherry Derr-Wille

Published by Rogue Phoenix Press, LLP
Copyright © 2021

ISBN: 978-1-62420-602-3

Credits
Cover Artist: Designs by Ms G
Editor: Amanda Armstrong

Dedication

I would like to dedicate this book to my friends and fans who encourage me and keep me writing. Also to my husband, Bob Wille, who understands my need to put the written word down and is my rock when those words are flowing.

Prologue

"I'm scared to death about this virus. From what my husband said, he suffered greatly before his death. I've had a premonition about this spreading not only to the U.S. but to the entire world," Caroline said. "Do you really think you can help me?"

The technician at the Cryogenics Lab examined the paperwork Caroline filled out earlier. "It looks like you're a good candidate for our services, Ms. Lewis. So far you have no symptoms of the virus, making you an ideal choice. You do know our services don't come for free."

Caroline reached into her purse and pulled out a stack of hundred-dollar bills. "From what I've read, you charge twenty thousand dollars. I have that amount right here. If you think you're going to raise the price just because of this virus, I'll leave right now."

"Don't be hasty, Ms. Lewis. Although there has been talk about raising the price, because of the current situation, no one has acted upon it. The twenty thousand will completely cover it. We can set your appointment for four thirty tomorrow afternoon. How long do you want to be frozen for?"

Caroline thought for a moment. With the virus spreading throughout the world, she prayed a cure would be found within the next fifty years. "I think until March of 2070 should be sufficient time. I'll see you tomorrow."

She left the office, secure in the knowledge that by this time tomorrow, she would be freeze dried until this pandemic was eradicated once and for all.

~ * ~

"Are you out of your mind, Caroline?" her brother Jonathan asked when she arrived at his home for supper that evening. "How could you throw away twenty thousand dollars on something this foolish? Those guys are nothing but shysters. Who knows what will happen to you in that place? I'm not ready to lose my sister."

"I'm willing to take that chance. My premonition about this virus, combined with my compromised immune system, is almost a death sentence in and of itself. If I can wake up fifty years in the future and not have to worry about any of these health problems, it's worth a shot. You know my husband was in China when this thing broke out and he died there. Other than you, I have no one else I care about left. This is the ideal solution for me."

"It's your decision and your money. Who am I to stop you, other than being your baby brother? I wish you well and I hope the future you're looking forward to is everything you want it to be."

"The cost of what I'm planning to do is only minimal considering what I'm worth. I have a document I want you to sign. It will transfer all of my assets to you. All I ask is that you take a minute part of them and invest wisely, so I will have money to live on when they awaken me in fifty years. I promise, I will come back to you. You are much younger than me and I am certain you will still be alive in 2070. We will meet again."

Chapter One

Los Angeles 2120

"I don't know what you're looking to find here, Nick. Los Angeles has been a wasteland since the pandemic, combined with the forces of nature, destroyed everything and everyone on the west coast a hundred years ago."

"It has, Lori, but something tells me we will make a find of great importance here. It could set the archaeology community on its ear with the biggest discovery of this century. We've got another three hours of time before they're expecting us back at headquarters. Let's just take a look through the ruins of this building."

Lori looked at the sign above the ruined building in front of them. "Cryogenics? What do you think that means?"

Nick stopped in his tracks, pulling up the Internet on his watch. After typing in the word that seemed alien to both of them, he waited for the response. "Let's see, it says that during the late twentieth and early twenty-first century, cryogenics was the freezing of human bodies to be awakened in the future when there was hope there would be a cure for some of the diseases plaguing the planet at that time. From what it says here, the quacks that promised eternal life through freezing the body in liquid nitrogen made a bundle off the people who came to them. It says here that people paid ten thousand dollars in the beginning and it went to twenty thousand dollars after the turn of the century. By the time the pandemic was at its peak, the price skyrocketed to over fifty thousand dollars. The people who were promoting this crap became millionaires overnight, for all the good it did them."

Lori thought about this history she'd learned, not only in high school but in college. The pandemic of 2020 had encompassed the world within a matter of weeks and disappeared just as quickly. With the world in chaos, it was the ideal time for World War III to be launched. Before it could, natural disasters wreaked havoc on both the east and west coasts of the United States, leaving millions of their citizens dead or dying. Now, a hundred years later, the government had declared the areas safe for the archeological teams to come in to reap the benefits of the knowledge from one hundred years ago in the hopes of keeping something like this from happening again.

"Okay, it won't hurt to go in there," Lori conceded. "It could prove quite interesting."

Carefully, they picked their way through the ruins of what once must have been a beautiful building. The lobby still sported a spectacular marble floor with the remains of what once must have been a receptionist desk. In front of them a spiral staircase led to a now non-existent second floor. To the right of it were stairs leading to what must have been a basement.

With trepidation, they made their way down the steps. Without the sunlight that illuminated the upper floor, they each switched on their flashlights as well as the lamps on their hardhats. As they did, they saw several chambers, with decaying bodies of men and women inside of the glass protective doors that looked like they cracked sometime over the past century, allowing the nitrogen gas to leak out and destroy them.

"So much for preserving eternal life," Lori quipped. "All they got for their tens of thousands of dollars was just as dead as anyone else. What a scam."

"Maybe not. Look here, this one is really well preserved. We'd better radio the team and see if anyone knows how to reverse this process. Think of the possibilities if we could resurrect a woman from 2020 or maybe before."

"I think you're right about 2020. There's a tag on the outside of her chamber and it says her name is Caroline Lewis and she was frozen on March 17, 2020."

It didn't take long for Nick to hurry up the stairs in order to make contact with their base camp. While he did, Lori continued to look at not only the decaying bodies, but the perfectly preserved body of the woman named Caroline drew her like a magnet.

"Why did you do it, Caroline?" she asked aloud, knowing she wouldn't get an answer.

As she continued to look around, she found a cabinet with several three ring binders in it. Being careful with the binders, she finally found one with the name of Caroline Lewis printed on the spine of the book.

She'd just pulled it out when Nick reappeared.

"I got a hold of Dr. Jamison and she is researching how to handle this. She said she should be here within the hour. Our instructions are to stay and guard this find until she gets here. I have a feeling this discovery is going to make us as famous as the archaeologists who discovered King Tut's tomb back in the early twentieth century."

"If I remember my history correctly, they all fell victim to a curse the ancient Egyptian put on Tut's tomb. I hope there isn't any kind of curse out on Caroline."

"Now you're being paranoid. Curses were things from ancient history and the dark ages. People were too advanced in the twenty-first century to believe in those things."

Lori agreed with Nick. There were no such things as curses but the three-ring binders she'd found in the file drawer could shed some light on the people in the damaged cryogenics chambers.

"I found these binders. The only one I took out was the one with Caroline's name on it. Since we have to wait for Dr. Jamison, we might as well see what it says about our sleeping beauty."

Lori opened the book and smiled to see the pages were encased in protective plastic. At least they wouldn't be too fragile to be touched.

"Caroline Lewis, female, forty-two years of age, no sign of the virus. Even though she suffered from breast cancer in 2017, she is cancer free," she read aloud. "It also says she paid twenty thousand dollars to the facility for her chance at eternal life. She wanted to be reawakened in

2070. Oh well, Caroline, you're only about fifty years overdue. I wonder how you will react to the state the world is in today."

Nick nodded his agreement. "We should take the remainder of the binders back to headquarters. They could be a treasure trove of information about the others who weren't as lucky as Caroline."

Lori agreed and started trying to figure out how they would be able to transport these important documents without a box or anything else to put them in.

~ * ~

Doctor Kirsten Jamison studied the information about cryogenics she found on her computer. While she'd been in college, she studied the ancient practice. She'd doubted it was anything more than an urban myth. Now after what Nick and Lori had discovered in the ruins of one of the buildings in what was once Los Angeles, they had debunked the urban myth theory.

Confident she could successfully reverse the process, she prepared to go out to the location where Nick and Lori made the discovery. Her hands shook as she packed her bags with the equipment her research told her would be necessary to reverse the effects of the cryogenics chamber.

Even though she'd never put much stock in the stories about cryogenics, she did recall the stories her grandmother often told her about her great-grandfather's sister, Caroline Lewis. According to what her grandmother told her, Caroline had been distraught over the loss of her husband who had been in China at the outbreak of the 2020 pandemic and died before he could return to the States. At the time she thought she had nothing to live for and went to the cryogenics facility. After her disappearance, the natural disasters began and Kirsten's great-grandfather took his family to the Midwest when the evacuation order had been issued. No one knew what happened to Great Aunt Caroline Lewis. Had she gone through with her plans to be frozen alive or had she lost her life during the disasters? It was one of those family legends that would forever be a mystery.

Outside of her office, her hovercraft pilot waited for her. She knew he wasn't thrilled about flying through the ruins of what was once Los Angeles, but they'd all signed on for this assignment. There were dangers, even mutant animals that roamed the streets of the long-forgotten city, but those were things that archaeologists had been dealing with for years all over the globe. In the past it had been curses on mu-mmies as well as snakes with the venomous bites. These new perils were just as real, forcing everyone who traveled to the area to be well-armed against whatever they might encounter.

"Are you sure you want to go into the inner city, Doctor?"

"That's where Nick and Lori have made the find. I can't very well examine the artifacts if I don't go there myself."

"I understand. I have my laser pistol as well as my rifle loaded, in case we should need to use them. I just hope Nick and Lori are all right. Even though they're armed, they could be in danger."

"From what Nick told me, what they found is in the basement of the ruins of a building. I doubt any animals would be going down a flight of stairs. There certainly isn't any food for them down there. I've heard most of them have retreated to the forests and the mountains."

Her pilot, Alex, nodded his agreement and they took off for the fifteen-minute flight to the area where they knew they would find Nick and Lori.

As they made their way through the now ruined streets of what was once a great city, Kirsten remembered the old pictures she'd found in her grandmother's attic when they cleaned out the house. Some of them were dated during the twentieth century, long before the pandemic or the natural disasters changed life as everyone knew it. The one picture that always drew her back to the old albums was of her great-grandfather, Jonathan Evers, and his sister, the mysterious Caroline Lewis. In the picture was Caroline's husband, Adam, along with great-grandmother Trudy Evers. They stood in front of a large home with well-groomed lawn as well as beds of colorful flowers. The date on the back of the picture was April 2016.

They must have thought they were living in paradise. What a difference those pictures are from the devastation we see now.

The hovercraft landed and parked next to the craft Kirsten knew Nick and Lori took out earlier in the day. The information she received from Nick told her that from here on she would have to go on foot, as there was so much debris there was nowhere closer to park their vehicles.

Alex flanked her as they made their way through the deserted streets of what was once the mecca of the entertainment world. As soon as she saw the sign denoting the cryogenics building, she turned to Alex. "This has to be the place."

Together they went into what had once been the lobby, turned on their flashlights, and made their way to the basement storage room.

"Dr. Jamison, it's good to see you," Nick said.

"I had to see what you have. From the condition of most of these bodies, I can see none of them survived. You did say there was one in perfect condition. Where will I find her?"

Lori got up from her seat at the desk where several three-ring binders were spread out. "She's over here," she said. "We do have a name for her. It's Caroline Lewis. I have all of her information in this binder. They certainly did keep good records on all of the people they put into a state of suspended animation."

"C-Caroline Lewis? Are you sure?"

"Positive. I have all the information on her right here and her name along with the date she was put in the tube is on the front of it. Does it mean something to you?"

"That's the name of my great aunt, the sister of my great-grandfather. I thought the stories about her visiting the cryogenics facility were just that; stories. She disappeared and no one seemed to know whatever happened to her."

Kirsten stepped around Nick and Lori to stare into the face of the woman whose picture had haunted her ever since she found it. Although she appeared older and thinner than the picture, this was definitely her great aunt. She took a deep breath, before she started the procedure she'd researched earlier. If her research was right, Caroline Lewis would slowly awaken, be disoriented, and regain full use of her body within a couple of hours. Of course, they didn't have the luxury of waiting for a couple of hours. Once she was awake, they would have to transport her back to headquarters, where she could be examined under better conditions than the remains of a crumbling building.

"Alex, I want you to help Nick take these binders out to his hovercraft. Lori, you'll have to stay here and help me."

Nick and Alex nodded and started taking armloads of binders back up to where the hovercrafts were parked.

"Did you check to see if there were any other survivors?" Kirsten asked.

"I don't know how it happened, but this was the only chamber that wasn't disturbed. If this is your great aunt, how do you think she'll adjust to waking up fifty years later than she thought she would?"

"Time will tell, but that's something we don't have now. I can reverse the process but it's hard telling if she will wake up immediately. At any rate, we have to get her back to headquarters as soon as we can. There we have the medical facility to take care of her that we don't have here."

From the notes Lori found in another of the binders, Kirsten started the process to awaken Caroline. There were some tense minutes waiting for the chamber to open. She certainly didn't know what she expected to find. Would the body turn black once the liquid nitrogen was released as had the other bodies, or would the controls take over and prevent something like that from happening. When the proper procedures were put in place, everything should go according to the plans of the original people who ran this facility in 2020.

She listened as the seal released and slowly the lifegiving oxygen reached the lungs of its lone occupant. Kirsten watched as Caroline's chest rose and fell with the breathing she hadn't done in over one hundred years.

Knowing complete awareness would not return for some time, Kirsten waited for Nick and Alex to return. Between the two of them they would have to carry the semi-conscious woman back to where their hovercrafts were parked.

"We put the binders in Nick's craft," Alex said. "Do you want us to make another trip with the rest of them?"

"Lori and I can get them. You need to take Caroline and put her in our hovercraft. We need to get her back to the lab so she can have access to the hospital facilities."

Kirsten watched as Alex and Nick lifted the bed on which Caroline and been lying inside the chamber and used it like a stretcher to transport her out to the hovercraft. Once they were on their way up the stairs, she and Lori picked up the remaining binders and carried them out of the basement. Luckily, they were able to illuminate the darkness with the headlamps on their hardhats while they attached their flashlights to their belts, freeing up their hands.

"That's the last of them, at least from the first drawer. I didn't get into the lower ones."

"I have a feeling there will be other archaeologists coming back here several times in the future, Lori. We can retrieve the rest of the files later or even send out another team to bring them back to headquarters. For now, I'm anxious to get Aunt Caroline back where she can be made comfortable."

Chapter Two

Caroline felt a strange sensation. She was aware of people talking around her, but was still out of it enough that she couldn't understand what they were saying. It was possible that it was now 2070 and she'd been awakened by the doctors and technicians who ran the cryogenics facility.

Not quite ready to open her eyes just yet, she luxuriated in the warmth which was in direct contrast to the cold of the cryogenics bed when she was first going into a state of suspended animation.

One of the voices sounded vaguely familiar and she thought perhaps it belonged to her sister-in-law, Trudy, but that couldn't possibly be so. Fifty years in the future, Trudy would be in her late eighties and the voice sounded much younger than that.

She tried to open her eyes but her eyelids refused to do as she wanted them to do. *They've been closed for so long, maybe they don't remember how to open.*

"I can see eye movement. I think she's beginning to come around."

The voice wasn't the one she thought belonged to Trudy. Maybe that was just part of her befuddled mind playing tricks on her.

"Can you hear us, Aunt Caroline?"

Aunt Caroline? Who would be calling me that?

"If you can hear me, can you lift a finger?"

Caroline wondered if her finger would respond since her eyes refused to open. Using every ounce of strength in her body, she raised the thumb of her right hand. At least she thought she raised it. Her mind told her to raise it, but did the body part respond? She prayed it did.

"Did you see that, Dr. Jamison? She raised her right thumb. She's coming out of it."

Caroline felt the compression of a blood pressure cuff on her right arm. How did they know not to use her left arm? Maybe that was in the paperwork she filled out at the facility before they approved her for the procedure.

"Her blood pressure is one forty over seventy. It's a little high, but for her age it's not bad. Her temperature has come up in the last hour. It's almost up to normal. That's a good sign."

Dr. Jamison? When did Trudy become a doctor? When did she change her name?

Almost without warning, her eyes opened. The woman dressed in hospital scrubs had a resemblance to Trudy, but she was much younger than the Trudy, Caroline remembered.

"Trudy?" Caroline managed to whisper.

It came as a surprise as to how hoarse her voice sounded.

"Trudy was my great-grandmother. My name is Kirsten Jamison."

"You can't be…I mean Trudy might have a great granddaughter but you're too old to be…"

"The year is 2120. My great-grandmother has been dead for over fifty years. I don't remember her, since she died before I was born, but my grandmother told me stories about her and when grandma passed away, I found a lot of old pictures in her attic."

"Did you say 2120? I was supposed to be brought back in 2070. What happened?"

The strength that was returning to her voice came as a surprise. She'd been told when she came around, she would be back to normal within a matter of hours.

"There's a lot you don't know. Over seventy years ago there was a major natural disaster. It's only been in the last five years that's we've been able to get back into any of the areas along the east and west coasts of the United States?"

"How could they have let me sleep that long? I-I was due to wake up fifty years ago," Caroline protested.

"Please try to stay calm. It's going to take more than a few minutes to explain everything to you. I can tell you how lucky you are. There were many others who were not as lucky as you are. There were many other bodies that were in various states of decay since they didn't receive the proper care when they were awakened. To be truthful, although I studied this in medical college, cryogenics were considered nothing more than an urban myth. The discovery of the facility, as well as being able to bring you back, is one of the major archeological finds of the twenty-second century."

"This is so mind boggling. Is there still a United States?"

"I know you have a lot of questions, but they can wait. For now, there is still a United States, but both the east and west coasts are basically wastelands. The same can be said for all the countries of the world bordering on the Atlantic and Pacific Oceans. When the disasters hit, they were felt all over the world. We can talk more about this later. For now, I need to have you get up and take a few steps before we bring you some dinner. The information from the binders we retrieved says you need to get your muscles moving first. Once you're up and mobile it will be time to reintroduce food to keep up your energy."

Slowly, Caroline sat up, with the assistance of Dr. Jamison and the other woman in the room. At first the room spun, but the longer she sat up, the steadier she became. Within about five minutes, she felt steady enough to allow her feet to touch the floor.

"Not bad for a one hundred-and-forty-something-old gal," she said.

"To be truthful, no matter how many years have passed, you're still only forty-two. The ageing processes ended when you entered the chamber and went into suspended animation. According to your papers, you had cancer. I haven't had time to do a thorough examination, but we'll be checking all of that when you're up to having a scan. For that we will have to be flying you to Chicago. The rest of the family will be anxious to meet you."

The rest of the family? Of course, after one hundred years,

Jonathan and Trudy's kids would have married and had kids of their own. I will miss my brother, but I'll have a whole new generation to meet and get to know.

With great difficulty, Caroline took one step after another until she walked all the way from the bed where she had awakened to the small table across the room. For taking her first steps, she was rewarded with a plate of food. Although she would have ordered a steak or maybe lobster, she was content with the plate of mashed potatoes, a small grilled chicken breast and a cup of applesauce.

"No wine?" she asked.

"Not until you have had a complete physical. Trust me, once we get back to Chicago and the family, you'll have all the partying you can handle."

As good as the food looked, Caroline was only able to eat one or two bites of each thing on the plate.

"I thought I would be hungrier. I feel like I've eaten a ten-course meal."

"You did well for your first meal. I have no doubt that your appetite will come back, but for now, you've done great. You need to get some rest. In the morning we're going to be flying back to Chicago. You're in for a lot of changes."

Caroline was surprised as how tired the minimal activity she'd engaged in left her. After sleeping for a hundred years, she thought she would never have to sleep again. She no more than closed her eyes than she fell into a deep and dreamless sleep.

~ * ~

Kirsten watched as the woman who was so familiar yet at the same time so alien quickly fell into a deep sleep.

One hundred years ago, Caroline went into the world of suspended animation in a world filled with chaos. Before the pandemic of 2020, people traveled freely to all the areas of the globe. It had been a time of plenty that soon became one where people hoarded everyday necessities, making rationing and great shortages the normal at many stores. People were told to not leave their homes and to go into isolation.

Was that the reason Caroline decided to go to the cryogenics facility? If so, it would have been a last-ditch measure that was completely unnecessary. Within a little over a year, a vaccination had been developed and the disease had been eradicated.

If it hadn't been for the disasters, the world would have gone back to normal, but what was once the norm was no longer what anyone remembered from the past.

"Oh, Aunt Caroline, I hope you can adjust to this world where you have awakened," she whispered. "I can hardly wait to have you tell me what your life was like before the pandemic and disasters changed everything."

Chapter Three

When Caroline again awoke, she was more aware of her surroundings. She was still clad in the hospital gown she'd worn when she first entered the state of suspended animation. For a moment, she thought of the beautiful wardrobe she left behind in her Beverly Hills home. She longed to put on her designer jeans and a form-fitting top, but was certain none of those things survived the natural disasters Dr. Jamison told her about when she first awoke.

With less trepidation, Caroline opened her eyes. Bright sunlight came through the window to her left. At the desk, in the corner of the room, she saw Dr. Jamison, making notes on what looked like a medical chart. She knew the notes were about her and the progress she was making.

"Good morning," Dr. Jamison chirped as though she had eyes in the back of her head.

"How did you know I was awake?" Caroline asked.

"I could tell you I'm psychic, but that would be a lie. I have this handy mirror to monitor you."

She pointed at a mirror positioned in front of her desk and just a little above her head.

"Oh, I see. What are the chances I can find some clothes to wear?"

"We don't have much here, but I have a pair of scrubs that you can wear until we get you to Chicago where we'll be able to build you a proper wardrobe."

"That sounds good, but what will I use for money? It seems to me I signed everything I owned over to my brother when I made the decision to go to the cryogenics facility. The people there assured me the twenty thousand dollars I paid would be used to purchase a new wardrobe. Something tells me the money has been spent and there are no clothes for me to wear. Of course, I asked my brother to invest some of my money, but I'm certain none of that is left."

"You're right, but my great-grandfather prayed until the day he died for your return. He took all of your assets and sold them. He also protected your money and transferred it to a bank in Chicago, when they relocated. Over the years it's been a family joke because no one thought you would ever return to claim it. Now that my great grandparents and grandparents are gone, my mother and father have been administering your money. They've also been investing wisely. I don't think you will have to worry about money for the rest of your life. Throughout the years, there have been many charitable donations made in your name, including a donation to one of the local hospitals for a new pediatric ward that carries your name."

"I'm completely overwhelmed. Only Jonathan would do such a thing. If someone had put me in charge of that much money, I don't know if I would have put the money aside or spent it. To be honest, I wasn't all that sure he would invest the money. Even if he hadn't, I was assured there would be money for me from the facility. How do you think your family will react to my return from the dead?"

"I talked to them last night and they are excited about meeting you. They've made plans to meet us at the spaceport when we arrive later today."

I hope I'm up to meeting this new branch of my family. These people will be strangers even though we all share the same DNA.

Kirsten left the room, giving Caroline the privacy necessary to change from the hospital gown to the scrubs. Even though they were a bit too big, she felt more comfortable with her body being completely covered. She wished she had some proper underwear, but as her mother always said, "beggars can't be choosers." Kirsten assured her she had enough money to shop at the most expensive stores on the Miracle Mile in Chicago, so a few hours, or maybe days, of being uncomfortable would be worth it.

She wondered what the style of the current day would be. She'd only seen Kirsten and her assistant since her awakening. They wore scrubs so she had no idea what she would even be shopping for.

Once she was dressed in the scrubs, she slipped her feet into the slippers that Kirsten called slides. She no more than finished, when Kirsten returned with a tray carrying her breakfast.

The tray, with a covered plate, reminded her of the food she'd eaten when she was hospitalized during her cancer treatments. She took off the cover and was pleased to see bacon, scrambled eggs and toast, along with juice and coffee.

"This looks like what I used to eat when I was…I mean before the pandemic. I guess food doesn't change that much."

"Fifty years ago, you might not have said that. The world was recovering and supplies were in short supply. It took the efforts of the scientists and farmers all over the world to bring back the supplies we once took for granted. Today, we are thriving, not only as a nation but also throughout the world."

"What about aliens? I mean, back in the day, we were all watching the sky looking for flying saucers."

Kirsten laughed. "They did land, but not until after the natural disasters. They were some of the scientists who helped the planet get back on track with both the food supply and the economy."

"I see. Does the United States still have a president?"

"Yes, but there are no longer political parties. Everyone is an independent and people vote for the candidate rather than the party. It has worked out well for the past fifty years. Before that, the party system almost drove what was left of the United States into wrack and ruin. When it was one party against the other, there were no winners and everyone suffered. Once the current form of government was established, everything turned around. Many other countries around the globe adopted the same form of government. Things seem to be running very smoothly and there hasn't been an outbreak of war in over thirty years."

Caroline could hardly believe what her niece was telling her.

Before the pandemic, the country was divided between Democrats and Republicans and war seemed to break out in a different area every few days.

~ * ~

It was well past noon when they made their way to the spaceport. While Caroline expected to see the bustling activity she was used to seeing at LAX, she was surprised to see minimal congestion. Rather than the big jetliners of the twenty and twenty first centuries, she gasped at the sight of what looked like one of the flying saucers people talked about.

"Are we going to fly in that?"

Kirsten laughed. "I've seen enough old movies with my dad to realize this wasn't what you were expecting. This type of transportation is much more efficient than the planes you remember. They're run on solar power rather than jet fuel so there are no emissions. Even when the sun isn't out, the power is stored within the internal batteries, so they are always ready to use. It has also cut flying time. In the old days it would take about four hours to get to Chicago from here, but with these craft, the time is cut to an hour."

"Just where is here?"

"We aren't too far from what used to be Los Angeles. I think in the old days it was called Needles. Today we call it the Southern California Research Area. There are many such facilities up and down the east and west coast, trying to see what we can find and how we can regenerate the land to be able to repopulate the areas sometime in the future."

Caroline shook her head. How could so much of the country be in such ruin that it was uninhabitable? It was almost inconceivable, but of course, she had awakened one hundred years in the future where everything was completely different from what she remembered.

It took a few minutes for the crew to be ready for them to board the vehicle that would take them to Chicago.

"I should warn you," Kirsten began, "once we get to Chicago, you might feel a bit like a lab rat. I'm told you'll be transported to a hospital where our doctors, as well as the scientists, can examine and question you. Since you had cancer before the pandemic began, your treatment, at least what you remember of it, will be of great value."

Caroline searched her memory for those dark days in 2017 when she'd been diagnosed with cancer not once but twice within six months. "I don't know what they want to know. My breast cancer was very rare. I don't think I reacted as well as I could have because I was very sick throughout the chemo treatments. Luckily, radiation was much better."

"You said you were diagnosed twice. What was the second cancer?"

"It was thyroid cancer. Luckily, it was found early. They were able to remove it completely and there were no other treatments needed. It was stage one, whereas my breast cancer was stage three. I had great doctors and once I finished all my treatments, I was proclaimed cancer free.

"My husband and I decided we were blessed. Blessed, that is, until he had to take a business trip to China. He was there when the pandemic broke out. Not only was he one of the first ones to contract it, but he was among the first ones to die from it. I was devastated. I didn't want to wait to die from the same disease, so that's when I looked into the possibility of cryogenics. I had heard the facilities were raising their prices. Since the going rate was twenty thousand dollars, that was what I took with me. I was certain the tech I talked to definitely wanted to charge me more, but I stood my ground. I know my brother thought I was completely out of my mind, but at least I didn't get caught up in the hysteria of Covid-19."

During the telling of her story, Caroline hardly realized the craft they were traveling in had taken off. She and her husband did a lot of traveling during their marriage, but she'd never been on a flight this smooth or silent.

"I guess I didn't realize we'd even taken off," she said.

"I know, isn't it great. I've heard stories about what air travel was like a hundred years ago and I much prefer the way things are today."

Caroline studied her great niece. "You know quite a bit about world history. Is that something everyone in this new world knows?"

"Hardly. My dad is a history buff. I watched enough old movies with him that when I went to college, I majored in medicine but I also carried a double major in world history, at least what there was of it. Even though I always wanted to be a doctor, I flirted with the idea of teaching history on the college level. Of course, medicine won out, because the world needed more doctors than they did historians. History isn't the most important thing these days. I still keep up on it, but will never put it to use, other than for my own personal satisfaction."

"We will be landing in Chicago within the next fifteen minutes. Please do not take off your seatbelts."

The announcement came as a surprise to Caroline. "Have we been flying for an hour already?"

Kirsten nodded. "I'm glad we had so much to talk about. It certainly made the trip seem to go faster. Before we left, I contacted my parents. They should be at the spaceport to meet us once we disembark."

The vertical landing was just as smooth as the lift off and flight had been. Within minutes of landing, they were walking down the jetway to where Kirsten's family, along with doctors and scientists were waiting for them.

"This isn't O'Hare or Midway. Where are we?"

"Those airports became obsolete when these new crafts took over the industry. This facility was built in what used to be Niles, Illinois. They can accommodate as many passengers per day as both O'Hare and Midway used to, only more effectively."

"Why were we the only passengers on our flight?"

"Because you're big news. This flight was a chartered one. The scientific community didn't want your discovery to be made public knowledge until they can do a complete evaluation of your medical status."

"That's something that bothers me. Why couldn't you do the medical evaluation?"

"I am a doctor, but at our outpost we didn't have the equipment they have in the larger hospitals here. I will be by your side for as long as it takes. The reason we couldn't leave until late afternoon was because I had to wait for my replacement to be sent out from Philadelphia."

Carolyn nodded and braced herself to meet the people who were waiting for her.

~ * ~

"What do you mean we can't take my daughter and my aunt to our home for the night?" Tom Jamison asked. "We're family, for god's sake."

"We know you are, Mr. Jamison. You have to understand, finding Caroline Lewis alive is the discovery of the twenty-second century. What you don't understand is, since the raising of Jesus from the dead, we have never brought anyone back to life after three days, to say nothing of a hundred years. Her discovery has to remain top secret until we can finish our examinations. We certainly don't want her exploited like the findings from King Tut's tomb were."

Tom shook his head. All his life he'd heard about the mysterious Caroline Lewis. Now that she would be landing soon, he wouldn't be able to take her to his home in order to get to know her and solve the family mysteries surrounding her disappearance over a hundred years ago.

The arrival of the chartered flight was announced and Tom elbowed his way to the front of the assembled crowd to be one of the first ones to see this long-lost family member.

~ * ~

Caroline had to look twice. If she hadn't been told her brother Jonathan passed away many years ago, she would have sworn the man standing at the front of the group gathered in the greeting area was him.

"That's my dad," Kirsten said. "He has an uncanny resemblance to Great-grandfather Evers, doesn't he? I should know I've studied the old pictures enough to see it. I guess we're both throwbacks to our ancestors."

"You certainly are. I would have sworn that was Jonathan waiting for me. Guess it was just wishful thinking."

With Kirsten by her side, she walked toward the group of men and women who were waiting for them.

"Ms. Lewis, I'm Dr. Kyle Andrews. Along with Dr. Jamison, I will be in charge of your care while you're at the hospital in Chicago."

"I'm pleased to meet you, doctor, but I would appreciate some time to see my family before I'm whisked away to some hospital to be poked and prodded."

The look on Dr. Andrew's face was priceless. Was it possible he wasn't used to one hundred and forty-two-year-old women talking back to him?

"Aunt Caroline, I'm Tom Jamison. My maternal grandfather was Jonathan Evers, your brother."

"The introduction wouldn't have been necessary. The two of you could easily have been twins. I feel as though I'm with him again. Will I be staying with you until I find a place of my own?"

"We were hoping so, but it seems Dr. Andrews and these scientists have other ideas. Hopefully, they will allow us to take you shopping for more appropriate clothing than hospital scrubs and slides."

Caroline noticed the scowl that crossed Dr. Andrews' face.

"I don't think…"

"Well, I do," Caroline interrupted. "In my day, I was considered a fashionista and my wardrobe didn't have one pair of hospital scrubs in it. You can run your tests, but I must insist on replenishing my wardrobe. I can assure you I don't have any despicable disease. If I had I would have never been a candidate for cryogenics, would I?"

"That is the problem, Ms. Lewis. We don't know anything about people being brought back from cryogenics. As far as we know no other people have ever been resurrected. We have to make certain you are healthy. We can make arrangements for one of the stores in the area to bring over a selection of clothing for you to at least choose the beginning of a wardrobe. Being at the hospital, you won't need much."

"What you don't seem to understand, doctor, is that I will need everything from undergarments to the latest fashions. I don't even know what the women in the twenty-second century consider fashionable. The only way I can do that is to go shopping for myself. I also need a bra fitting, unless women these days don't wear such things. Do you think that's something you can handle?"

Caroline's comment seemed to break the tension, bringing laughter from everyone in the group. Dr. Andrews' temperament seemed to go from confident to completely embarrassed.

"This is highly irregular, but having a wife of my own, I do understand your need for the proper wardrobe. I will put you into Dr. Jamison's care for the weekend, but you are to report to the hospital first thing on Monday morning."

She thought for a moment. "I don't even know what day this is. How many days does it give me to shop?"

"It's Thursday, Aunt Caroline," Thomas said. "That will give you Friday and Saturday to hit the stores with my wife and daughter. Since the natural disasters, our country has gone back to the religion of our forebearers. Shopping is done Monday through Saturday and all stores are closed on Sunday so people can attend church services."

"Now that is interesting. I heard my parents talk about how things were closed on Sundays, but I never thought I'd see the day that the merchants put church services in front of the almighty dollar. Since I don't have to be at the hospital until Monday morning, perhaps I can go to Sunday services with you."

"I wouldn't recommend that," Dr. Andrews said. "Since no one other than those of us in this room knows of your existence, I'm afraid you would be opening yourself to attention from the press."

"If no one knows about me, why can't I be introduced as a visiting out of town relative? No one outside of the family would know the name Caroline Lewis."

Dr. Andrews' response was an exasperated sigh. "I can see there is no use in arguing with you, Ms. Lewis. We will see you on Monday morning sporting the latest fashions and having worshiped with your family. I hold you responsible for your aunt's well-being, Dr. Jamison. If the wrong people get wind of what's going on, it will be on you and you alone."

The doctors and scientists filed out of the reception area, leaving Caroline alone with her family.

"This is so overwhelming," Caroline said. "I thought perhaps I would meet an older version of my brother and his wife. I never expected to find such an extended family."

"The rest of the family is waiting for you at home," Tom said. "I'm certain anything in my wife's wardrobe will fit you until she can take you shopping tomorrow."

~ * ~

Caroline marveled at the area they went through. She remembered the congestion of Los Angeles and thought the same would be true about the area around Chicago. Instead of the mass of concrete highways, the traffic was in the sky, as hovercrafts were now the accepted mode of transportation.

"Do these craft run on electricity?" she asked.

"Everything is run either on solar power or the power from the wind turbines. We learned many valuable lessons when the natural disasters shut down the power grids and threatened the oil supplies. The entire world is now run on these things, eliminating the many wars over those natural resources."

She nodded at Tom's explanation. Even a hundred years ago she thought the world was crazy for not utilizing the natural power sources that were free for the taking.

The hovercraft landed in front of traditional single-story home with a beautifully manicured lawn.

"You home reminds me of the house my brother had in L.A. Mine was much larger, but thinking back I don't know why my husband and I needed such a large place."

"Didn't you have children?" Kirsten asked.

Tears welled up in Caroline's eyes. "We had a daughter, but she only lived a few hours. After that, even though we tried, we were never able to conceive another child. My husband was in China on business and was looking into an international adoption when the Covid-19 outbreak first was detected. He was one of the first Americans to die in China. Unfortunately, it wasn't widely known because he was half Chinese, so wasn't thought to be an American. His death was what prompted me to look into the cryogenics. I didn't want to consider the chance of contracting the virus. I know it was selfish of me, but I felt so alone. I decided it was best if I went to sleep for fifty years and start fresh in 2070. Boy was I wrong."

Once in the house, Caroline was thrilled to meet more of the family. Tom's wife, Nora, was warm and welcoming.

"I had a call from Tom and he says you are ready to go shopping. For today, let's start in my closet. I'm certain we can find something that will be flattering to you. Tomorrow I will take you to all of my favorite stores. You'll be coming with us, won't you, Kirsten?"

"You know I will, Mom. I love your shopping trips. All of this happened so quickly, I didn't even get a chance to bring anything with me except the scrubs I've been wearing for weeks."

Nora's closet gave Caroline a look at what the fashions of the twenty-second consisted of. She was afraid they would be the bland colorless jumpsuits portrayed in various futuristic movies she'd watched over a hundred years earlier. The colors and prints that dominated Nora's wardrobe delighted her. She could see herself wearing anything in this beautiful walk-in closet.

After choosing a full skirt with a jewel-tone blouse, she was more than willing to shed the borrowed hospital scrubs. Even the shoes that lined one of the shelves were the right size and something she knew she would have purchased for herself.

"My clothes are more flattering on you than on me. I know we'll have great fun shopping tomorrow."

"Thank you. I hope I can find a place of my own soon. I don't like imposing on others."

"Nonsense. With Kirsten off to God only knows where with her work and our son living and working in Texas, we are suffering from empty nest syndrome. Kevin's room is crying for someone to take it over.

He and Kirsten are twins and with them both leaving home at the same time, we've been rattling around this place."

Nora took Caroline to a room that had once been the domain of a teenage boy. It was spacious and the closet was almost as large as the one in the master bedroom.

I could be comfortable here, at least until I adjust to this new world I'm now in. From what I've learned, the home where my husband and I were so happy is in ruins. It's time for me to recreate myself.

Chapter Four

The weekend ended far too soon to suit Caroline. The freedom of shopping and worshiping with her family made her dread going back to the hospital. Even so, a promise was a promise and she had never been one to go back on her word.

She was pleased when most of the examinations were done by Kirsten, rather than the pompous Dr. Andrews.

"You don't have a nipple on your left breast. Why is that?" Kirsten asked.

"My cancer was Paget's Disease. It hid under the nipple for three years before it was diagnosed. Everyone kept telling me it was a fat deposit and not to worry about it. It wasn't until the small lump grew to encompass three quarters of the nipple, that I went to a dermatologist and she did a punch biopsy. That's when I found out it was cancer. Unfortunately, by that time it was stage three and had invaded the lymph nodes under my left arm. Had it not gone that far, I could have gotten off with not having chemo. Anyway, when they took out the lump, they took off the nipple. I could have had one tattooed on but my husband and I talked about it and we decided it didn't make any difference to either of us. I told them as long as I had breasts, even though they were much smaller than they'd been for most of my life, I was happy."

"Oh, Aunt Caroline, you are so funny. What a fantastic outlook. As you'll learn, in the past hundred years we've made great strides in medicine. Cancer has been eradicated much like many of the diseases that were wiped out in the twentieth and twenty-first centuries."

"Now that's definitely a blessing. I wouldn't wish chemotherapy on anyone. I lost all of my hair, and had a terrible time with low white and red blood levels. Between being hospitalized with a low white blood count and having to have a transfusion when it was the red blood count that was also too low, I was one sick cookie. Thank goodness I didn't have the vomiting I'd heard about in the past."

She watched as Kirsten frantically jotted notes about everything she was telling her. With no more cancer in the world, perhaps it was best that people knew the horrors of the disease that was no longer a threat.

With the physical examinations finished, Caroline was proclaimed disgustingly healthy. It was then the scientists and archaeologists came to question her about what it was like to be put in a state of suspended animation and be frozen with liquid nitrogen for so many years.

"Did you have a near-death experience? Did you die and go to heaven?"

"I did not die. Therefore, I didn't have a near-death experience. As I think of it, I would have welcomed a trip to heaven to meet with my Lord. Unfortunately, it was as though I was merely asleep. When I awoke, it was to a new world, one of which I know nothing about."

~ * ~

At the beginning of her second week at the hospital, she was taken to a conference room for a press conference. She was ushered to a seat at the front of the room along with Kirsten, Dr. Andrews and two young people she didn't recognize. Assembled in front of them were reporters from the major networks as well as the local stations and newspapers.

"Ladies and gentleman," a man Caroline hadn't seen before began. "Two weeks ago, the husband and wife team of archaeologists, Nick and Lori Parker, were exploring the ruins of what was once Los Angeles. In their search, they came across a building with the word 'cryogenic' denoting what it was once used for. In the basement of the building they found the rotting remains of people who were frozen with liquid nitrogen, lying in the cryogenic beds.

"In the last bed, they found one perfectly preserved body. The name on the front of the bed was Caroline Lewis, who had been put into the chamber in March of 2020. Dr. Kirsten Jamison was called in to reverse the process of cryogenics and release Ms. Lewis from her one-hundred-year sleep.

"I will turn this over to Dr. Jamison and Dr. Andrews who have been caring for and examining Ms. Lewis."

"Thank you," Kirsten said, taking her place at the microphone. "With great thanks to the binders we found at the facility, I was able to safely open the cryogenic bed and release Ms. Lewis. For her it wasn't the awakening she'd planned, but one fifty years in the future from the date she agreed to.

"Along with the bodies, Nick and Lori also discovered a treasure trove of notebooks with statistics on each of the bodies in the beds. There was also one that detailed the exact procedure to open the chambers and that was the one I used for her reawakening."

Dr. Andrews took over the narrative telling the reporters about the physical condition of Caroline and pronouncing her to be in perfect health.

He ended his prepared speech by holding out his hand to Caroline. Even though she didn't like being in the spotlight, she got to her feet.

"Ms. Lewis," one of the reporters shouted out. "How are you finding life in the twenty-second century?"

"To be truthful, other than the first weekend after I arrived in Chicago, I haven't been anywhere except the hospital to experience much of anything. I did enjoy being able to shop for clothes that were of the current fashion and attend a church service. To be truthful, I didn't know if the people of this era were still practicing Christians. I am sad to know that my beloved California is no longer inhabitable."

"Were you surprised to be awakened fifty years later than you expected?" another reporter asked.

"I most certainly was. I hoped to be reconnected with my younger brother who would have been in his mid-eighties. It saddens me to think he has been dead for many years. Thankfully, he was able to move his family as well as his assets to Chicago before the natural disasters that hit the west coast."

After about fifteen minutes, the questions being asked of Caroline were finished. She was relieved when the questions were being directed to Lori and Nick.

The press conference lasted just over an hour. When at last the cameras were turned off, Caroline was told she was free to leave the hospital. She returned to her room and packed the few possessions she'd brought with her when she first checked in.

As she prepared to leave, Caroline realized she had no plans for the future. Tom and Nora assured her the assets her brother put aside in her name had increased so much she would be independently wealthy.

When she'd been married, she was content to be considered a wealthy woman who, working beside her husband, was able to support themselves in grand style. Now she wasn't so sure about being able to live the life of luxury. At the age of forty-two it was possible she could go back to school and learn a trade. If she didn't work maybe she could become involved in volunteer work.

She was still considering her options when there was a knock at the door. Before she could get to her feet, Tom and Nora entered the room.

"We watched your interview on the monitor in the day room of the hospital," Nora greeted her. "You were fabulous. I don't think I would have been able to answer all the questions the press asked you as calmly as you did."

"It probably wouldn't have gone so well if it hadn't been for Kirsten giving me a heads up about what she thought they might be asking me. In case you haven't figured it out, you have a very special daughter. She has certainly made my stay here in the hospital tolerable."

"We know how special she is. Unfortunately, now that you're being released from the hospital, she'll be going back to her research in the California area. She told us there were three more drawers filled with notebooks and she is anxious to read through them."

Caroline shook her head. "I thought she was a medical doctor. Why would these be of interest to her?"

Tom laughed. "I'm sure Kirsten has shared with you about her love of world history. She read several of the notebooks about the other occupants of the cryogenics beds and learned a great deal about what prompted them to pay the money to be frozen. She's hoping to perhaps find another location with cryogenic beds."

"It would be nice if she did, because then I would no longer be a one of a kind. How soon do you think she will have to leave to go back to California? Maybe I could go along with her and help..."

"Oh, no you don't," Tom interrupted. "I've waited all my life to meet my mysterious Aunt Caroline. I refuse to allow you to disappear so soon after your arrival."

"You two can talk about this later," Nora said. "I made reservations for us at my favorite restaurant and I refuse to be late. Caroline and I have to make plans for our shopping trip to the city tomorrow."

The more Caroline was with her nephew and his wife, the more she liked Nora. Had they met in the beginning of the twenty-first century she was certain they would have become fast friends.

Chapter Five

Although Caroline always considered herself a shopaholic, she realized she couldn't hold a candle to Nora. It hadn't taken long for Caroline to replenish her wardrobe. With that done, she saw no reason to patrol the stores, looking for things she didn't need.

"Are you ready to go shopping?" Nora asked at breakfast.

"Not today. I think I'm pretty much shopped out. I want to take today to decide what I want to do with the rest of my life. I can only do so much shopping. It was different when I was married and shopped to take care of my husband, but without him in my life, I have to find something more meaningful to do. Do you have any ideas?"

"Oh, good heavens no. In this day and age, true ladies no longer work. With everything that has happened over the years, women of the upper class are no longer necessary in the workforce."

"I noticed several women working at the hospitals I've been in since I woke up. Why are they still working?"

"They are either single or they don't belong to the upper classes. I realize my daughter works, but it wasn't something I approved of."

"That is indeed a shame. As I recall, my sister-in-law as well as my mother were well respected in their chosen fields. I didn't work outside of the home, but I was a partner in my husband's online company. I often thought it would have been for the best if I'd accompanied him on that final trip to China. At least we would have been together at the end of his life."

Nora shook her head, as though she had no understanding of what Caroline was saying. "Well, I wish you luck, but I have no idea what you think you'll find to occupy your time."

Nora finished the last of her coffee and prepared to leave the house for the day.

With nothing else to occupy her time, Caroline went into the room Tom used as a study and booted up his laptop. After putting in a search for volunteer positions, she was surprised to see the local library was looking for someone to work in the research department.

She wrote down the address and realized it was within walking distance of Tom and Nora's home. On one of her shopping trips with Nora, they'd passed the library and Caroline marveled at the fact such places still exhisted.

After taking a quick shower, dressing in one of her new outfits and putting on her makeup, she left a note on the table saying not to worry about her as she was on an outing. She assured them she would be home later.

~ * ~

The library was located in a stately old building. From the date on the cornerstone, she realized the building had been erected at the beginning of the twentieth century.

At least this building resembles the ones I remember. It will be like stepping back in time rather than existing in the futuristic-looking buildings I've found here.

People milled around the lobby as she made her way to the front desk.

"May I help you?" the woman at the desk asked.

"Yes, you may. I was browsing on the internet and saw you are looking for volunteers to work in the research department. Whom would I talk to about this position?"

"That would be Aaron Phillips. His office is at the end of this hall. I'm sure he will be delighted to see you, since the position had been advertised for several weeks now and no one has applied."

Caroline thanked the woman and went down the hall she

indicated. There were several offices, all with closed doors. The one with the name "Aaron Phillips, Director of Research" beside it stood with its door open.

"Mr. Phillips?" she asked, announcing herself. "I'm Caroline Lewis and I'm here to inquire about the volunteer position I found when I was looking on the Internet."

"Caroline Lewis? Are you the woman who was on the news a couple of weeks ago?"

"One and the same."

"I'm pleased to meet you, but I must ask why are you interested in working as a volunteer? There is no money in it."

Caroline laughed at his statement. "I assure you, Mr. Phillips, I'm not here because of the money or lack thereof. When I disappeared in 2020, my brother put aside my assets thinking I would be coming back for them. The family has been investing them ever since. I do not need the money, but I do need to do more with my time than go shopping on a daily basis. I feel I would be an asset to your department."

"I have a feeling you would. There is a group of people who meet here on a monthly basis. They're very interested in the ancient history of this country, in other words, the twentieth and twenty-first centuries, before the natural disasters changed the face of this country as well as that of all the countries bordering on the Pacific and Atlantic Oceans. I have a feeling you will be a font of information for them."

"Once a month is good, but I was hoping for more."

"Oh, there would be more. As much as the government want to think research is not essential, the call for it is almost overwhelming. I've been hoping for an assistant for several weeks. My last volunteer, who was extremely good at what she did, had to leave because her husband was relocated to North Dakota for his job."

Caroline smiled. "What would the hours be and how soon can I start?"

"It would be from ten to three every day, Monday through Friday, along with meeting with the history buffs once a month on Thursday afternoon from one to four. Would that be acceptable to you?"

"More than acceptable. Would it be possible to look around and get a feel for your department, Mr. Phillips?"

"You are eager. Well, if you're going to be working for me, I would appreciate it if you called me Aaron. That is of course, if I may call you Caroline?"

"That works for me, Aaron. I have to say this position is a godsend. I had no idea what I would be doing to keep myself occupied in this new world. Hopefully, you can fill me in on what I've missed over the past one hundred years."

After shaking hands with the man who was to become her new boss, she followed him around the library building. It was much like the one she remembered frequenting in Los Angeles. It encompassed three floors, with the research department located on the first floor, next to the Great Writers of History section of books.

She was surprised when she saw books written by some of her favorite writers from the twenty-first century. "I can't believe you have books by William Mathis, Lorna Collins, Marilyn Meredith and Maxine Douglas. Back in the day, they were internet authors and their books were called trade paperbacks. I'm surprised to see them in hard copy."

"From what I'm told, these were popular authors even after their deaths. Once they passed, their books became more sought after, and traditional publishing houses bought the rights from the surviving families and put them out in hardcover. This section of the library gets a lot of traffic because people are interested in what life was like in the old days."

"What about the authors of today?"

"Oh, they're out there, but most of them are self-published and I'm afraid not as well edited as the older authors were. There are some good ones as well. We will see a whole section of their work next."

Caroline nodded, and reluctantly left the section with the authors she considered her friends. Most of the books were ones she'd read and kept in her at home library. In the future she would be visiting this section again.

The full tour of the library took over an hour. Once they returned to Aaron's office, Caroline knew she would enjoy working not only here, but also with Aaron.

"Can I walk you to your vehicle?"

"I don't have a vehicle, and even if I did, I would have no idea how to fly it. I've been staying with my niece and nephew. They live within walking distance of the library."

Aaron smiled. "May I walk you home?"

"Oh, that wouldn't be necessary."

"Perhaps not, but it would be my pleasure. It's been a long time since I've had the privilege of spending the afternoon with such an interesting woman."

"Why Aaron, what would your wife say?"

"If she was still alive, she would say go for it. She was involved in a hovercraft accident five years ago. Her injuries were so severe, she died at the scene. I didn't even get a chance to say good-bye to her."

"I'm sorry. I can understand. I lost my husband at the beginning of the pandemic of 2020 while he was on a business trip to China. It was the reason I..."

"You don't have to explain. Grief can do some terrible things to a person."

~ * ~

Although the sun was still shining brightly, Caroline knew it was late when she and Aaron arrived at Tom's home.

"Thank you for seeing me home safely, Aaron. As you can see, I do live within walking distance of the library."

"It was my pleasure. I'm looking forward to seeing you tomorrow morning."

"Caroline, where have you been?" Tom said as he approached them from the front porch.

"Oh, Tom, I didn't mean to cause you any worry. I saw the library was looking for volunteers and I went down there to apply. I guess time got away from me. This is Aaron Phillips."

"I know who he is. It's good to see you, Aaron. I hope you plan to treat my aunt with the respect she deserves."

"You know I will, Tom. If my memory serves me correctly, you and Nora were very good friends of my late wife. I've missed seeing you since her passing. Of course, I haven't been to many social gatherings in the past five years."

Caroline exchanged glances between Tom and Aaron. She couldn't tell if there was animosity between the two of them or if Tom was being overprotective of her.

"I'll look forward to seeing you tomorrow," Aaron said, extending his hand to her. "It was good to see you again, Tom. Hopefully, we'll be seeing more of each other in the future."

The two of them shook hands and she watched as Aaron walked back toward the library.

"I didn't realize you wanted something other than shopping and relaxing in your life," Tom said.

"I thought I made myself clear on that subject. I have enjoyed shopping with Nora, but I need something more in my life. The volunteer position at the library is perfect for me. I love doing research and I feel like I'm among friends when I'm in the library. When I get to the point that I'm comfortable enough, I plan to start bringing home books to read. I realize that is something I have missed since I woke up. In 2020, I read several books a month."

"I just don't think you need to work. I told you the money that has been invested over the years is enough for you to live comfortably for the rest of your life."

"What you don't realize, Tom, is that I'm bored. In my other life, I had my husband and together we worked with his company. Even though I didn't have to work, I enjoyed it. I'm not working for money. This is an unpaid position. The payment I receive will be helping others and getting out on my own again."

By the time she finished speaking her mind, they were in the house, where Nora waited for them.

"I only caught a little of your conversation with Tom but I applaud you," Nora said. "This morning I couldn't understand why you didn't want to go with my friends and me shopping, but when we were out, they made me see that you're from a different time and place. I hope this position at the library is something you will enjoy."

"It's just the first step, Nora. Once I'm comfortable there, I want to look into getting my own place."

"You know you're welcome to stay here as long as you like," Tom said.

"I know I can, but I know how I would feel if we had taken a stranger into our home. A woman can only share her kitchen for just so long without resenting the presence of another woman. I love you both and am grateful for everything you have done, but I need to find my own way in this world."

This time, Nora stood and actually applauded Caroline. "You are a strong woman. I can understand your need to be on your own. I hope you will stay with us a while longer and when the time comes, I will be so excited to help you find and decorate a place of your own, just as long as you don't move too far from us."

Chapter Six

Life soon fell into a routine of helping Nora around the house before she left for work at the library. Her only disappointment was that she rarely had the opportunity to see Aaron on a daily basis. With her office down the hall from his, she remained busy from the time she arrived until she was ready to go home.

As usual when she arrived at work, she opened the computer program with her daily calendar and saw the notation regarding the meeting of the group who were interested in the world she had called home for the majority of her life.

She was surprised when someone knocked on her office door. "Enter," she said, without looking up to see who was there.

"Do you always allow people to come into your office without asking who is there?"

Caroline turned from the information on her computer screen to see Aaron standing in the doorway. "I guess I should have been a little more cautious, but I was engrossed in thinking about the meeting of the group that's set for this afternoon."

"That's what I came to talk to you about. I realize I've left you on your own since you've been here, but I was in conference with the library board. They have been hounding me for the past two weeks about my budget. They wanted a complete accounting and that has taken up most of my time. They even scrutinized my hiring you. I don't know what they thought, but I finally convinced them you were a volunteer and not being paid."

"I wondered why I didn't see you around as much as I thought I would."

"Anyway, today is the meeting of the group that are interested in your time period. What I forgot to tell you is they always go out to dinner after the meeting. I hope I'm not too late in mentioning it, so you can join us."

Caroline smiled. "I'm not exactly a social butterfly lately. I just have to contact Nora and let her know not to expect me home until later."

Aaron nodded and left her alone to make contact with Nora. Once he was gone, she activated the communications watch Nora insisted she purchase. It took a while for her to learn how to use it. She admitted it was much easier than using a phone or a computer. It meant instant connection as everyone always wore their watches.

"Caroline, is something wrong?" Nora asked as soon as her picture appeared on the screen of Caroline's watch.

"Nothing is wrong. I needed to let you know I won't be coming home for dinner tonight. This is the day I meet with the research group for the first time and they go out to eat after the meeting. Aaron apologized for not letting me know sooner, and he promised me he would bring me home afterward."

"I think that sounds wonderful. I was worried about your social life. Have a good time. I want to hear all about it when you get home."

The connection went dark and Caroline checked her emails to see what questions needed researching today.

~ * ~

Caroline hardly realized it was noon, until Aaron entered her office, carrying a takeout container from the cafeteria located in the basement of the library.

"I've been told you don't seem to take time for lunch. Considering the meeting will be starting in an hour, I took the liberty of bringing you something that we can share."

"Should I be worried about your selection?"

"I hope not. It's Chinese/American day and I know they make a great stir fry as well as delicious spring rolls. I also know the portions are enough to share."

"Have you been doing research about me?"

Aaron seemed to blush. "Guilty as charged. I did check and learned your husband was half Chinese. That said, I prayed you would share his love of Chinese/American cuisine."

"You were correct. It will be different eating it with silverware, since I used to be adept at using chopsticks."

"It's not a lost art. I brought chopsticks for both of us. I learned how to use them when I was a kid. My grandparents enjoyed going to one of the Chinese/American restaurants in their town and they insisted I learn how to eat like the owners did. After the pandemic as well as the natural disasters, there were many more ethnic restaurants that popped up around the country. With each of them, more and more people learned to eat like their hosts did."

Caroline unwrapped the chopsticks and tasted the stir fry. She was delighted with the taste of the food she'd loved over a hundred years earlier.

"Talk about healthy eating. I certainly enjoy this much more than some of the synthetic meals Nora prepares. These vegetables are excellent."

With their shared lunch finished, they made their way to one of the conference rooms on the third floor to await the arrival of the research group.

One by one the members of the group began to arrive. If they were curious about the stranger who was now joining them in their meeting, it didn't show.

"Welcome everyone," Aaron said. "I'm sure you've heard about the woman who was found in the cryogenic bed in the archaeological area of southern California. We are blessed to have had Caroline Lewis join our research department. She is thrilled to be able to attend your meeting and answer many of the questions I am certain you have for her. I have put name tags at each of your places, so if you would fill them out it will be easier for her to learn your names and be able to address each of your questions."

Caroline listened to the many comments around the table from those who were gathered for the meeting. When the chatter quieted down, she got to her feet.

"I am delighted to be with you today. I hope my one-hundred-year-old memory will be able to answer all of your questions."

"I'm a fashion designer," Suellen, a perky little blonde, began. "What did women wear in 2020?"

Caroline smiled at the question. At least this one was something she could easily answer. "Things were much more laid back. The big fashion statement, at least for me, was blue jeans. It was hard to find dresses unless I went to one of the secondhand shops. I am so pleased to see fashions going back to what they were during the mid-twentieth century. As much as I enjoyed the comfort of my jeans and sensible shoes, I did miss wearing dresses and heels."

She expected snickers from the men in the group. Instead, everyone seemed to be frantically taking notes.

"I am surprised to find out the styles we are wearing today are a throwback to over a hundred and fifty years ago. Here I thought my colleagues and I were creating original works."

"Oh, my dear," Caroline replied, "you must know there is no such things as original works. As I recall, I was once told there are only nine storylines when people are writing romance. It's just that the characters and locations are different. It's the same with fashion. Whatever is old is eventually new again, or as the younger generation from my time would say, 'what goes around comes around'."

For the next three hours, many more questions were asked and to Caroline's delight they were ones she could easily answer. Time seemed to fly and soon it was time for them to adjourn.

"Where have you decided to go for dinner tonight?" Aaron asked. "Caroline has agreed to be my guest and spend some quality time getting to know each of you better without having to answer any more of your questions."

Jason got to his feet. "We decided we would be going to the

French Bistro. I hope that will be some place you would enjoy, Ms. Lewis."

"It certainly would, but please call me Caroline. Ms. Lewis sounds more like an elderly school teacher. Although I am chronologically one hundred and forty-two years old, I stopped aging as soon as I went into suspended animation. Therefore, I am a healthy forty-two-year-old woman living in this new world that is as alien to me as my world would be for you."

Her comment brought laughter from everyone in the group, putting her immediately at ease with going out to dinner with these strangers she hoped to get to know better.

~ * ~

It was after eight when Aaron landed his hovercraft in front of Tom and Nora's house. The longer she was a citizen of the twenty-second century, the more accustomed she became to this silent and ecologically clean mode of transportation.

"It was a delightful evening," Caroline said, as she prepared to go into the house.

"I thought so as well. I would like to see you, socially, on a regular basis. Would that be acceptable to you?"

She smiled. "I was afraid you would think I would be too forward if I asked you the same thing. It is wonderful to have family in this time and place, but I need more in my life."

In the waning light of the late summer evening, Caroline saw a smile spread across Aaron's lips. "Since today is Thursday, would you be interested in going to the theatre with me on Saturday night? I hear there is a good production of a play that was popular just before the pandemic surfaced. It's called *Hamilton*. Have you heard of it?"

"I have. My husband and saw it when it was put on in L.A. We loved it. I will be anxious to see how close to the original script this new production will be."

"Good. I was afraid I would be stuck with two tickets. I'll pick you up at two on Saturday afternoon. That should give us time to go into the city, have an early dinner and be at the theatre for the seven o'clock performance."

Caroline was prepared to lean toward Aaron for a goodnight kiss, when he took her right hand in his and put it to his lips.

"I probably won't see you tomorrow, because I have an all-day meeting at one of our outlying branches. I look forward to seeing you on Saturday, dear lady."

Chapter Seven

For the first time, Caroline didn't look forward to going to the library to put in her volunteer hours. Even when she didn't see Aaron, she knew he was in the building. Today he was going to be at the outlying branches, and she knew she wouldn't see him in passing.

After checking her email and voicemail for questions that needed her expertise, she got to work. It didn't take long for her to find the answers to the various requests. With nothing else on her to do pile, she set about doing some research for questions she had about this new world.

The first search she did was on DNA. It came as a surprise to realize DNA profiles were built on every newborn baby. She was certain a DNA test had been performed on her when she was in the hospital for the many tests the officials deemed necessary.

Having watched the nightly news, she marveled at how few murders and rapes were being reported. When she asked Tom about it, he could give her no logical explanation. To be truthful, he questioned what she was even talking about.

With this new information, it was no wonder these crimes had been virtually eradicated. Even though DNA was in its infancy in the early twenty-first century, more and more crimes were being solved using the results of these tests. With everyone being tested and having those results in a national database, anyone would have to be stupid to commit a crime that could be so easily solved through the use of their biological signature.

The next thing she decided to check up on was Covid-19. Like so many other pandemics that flourished throughout the world over the centuries, it disappeared almost as soon as it was first detected. Unlike the bubonic plague of the middle ages, as well as the Spanish flu of the early twentieth century, doctors, scientists and researchers around the world worked together to find not only a cure but also a vaccine against this dreaded disease.

An alert of an incoming email interrupted her personal research projects. After reading the new post, she recognized the name of one of the members of the group meeting from the afternoon before.

The request was for what the group wanted her to talk about at their next meeting. In this world where there seemed to be no solved and unsolved murders, they were interested in the crime and violence of her time period. This was something she knew quite a bit about. Living in Los Angeles, she saw the results of those heinous acts not only through the newscasts, but all of the true crime dramas depicting dramatizations of many of these occurrences.

She took very little time in sending a reply saying she was excited about the prospect of such a discussion.

By three o'clock, Caroline was more than ready to return home. Between the research for patrons of the library and those for her own gratification, she found herself exhausted. At the end of the day, she was excited about the prospect of the weekend beginning. Saturday was the day she would, once again, see Aaron.

~ * ~

Nora greeted Caroline when she arrived back at the house. "Did you have a good day at work?"

"It was relatively quiet, so I did some research on things I wanted to know about life in the twenty-second century. I think you remember me questioning the lack of news about murders and rapes. I researched DNA and learned every baby is tested at birth and the information is put into a database. With that knowledge, anyone would be either stupid or a damned fool to commit a crime that could be immediately solved through DNA."

"I could have told you about that. I just thought it was something that had always been done."

"DNA analysis wasn't perfected until the 1990s and didn't become a popular thing to do until the early twenty-first century. Back then, people wanted to know where their ancestors came from and perhaps to find they were related to royalty. In many cases, people were looking for long lost relatives. There was even a TV show that helped people find birth family or people who had disappeared from their lives. Many of the participants on the show were children who had been adopted or people who had given up a child at birth to give them a better life."

Nora gave Caroline a look of astonishment at her story of life in a time Nora could not even imagine. "Are you saying people actually gave children away?"

"Back in the day, many couples couldn't have children and fertility clinics were expensive. Add to that the number of teenagers and other unmarried people having unprotected sex, adoption was the logical thing to do when there was an unwanted pregnancy or the parents were too young to become children raising children. Many of the adoptees were either unhappy about their adoptive parents or just curious about the people who gave them life. Sometimes the outcomes were good and other times things didn't work out for them."

They talked about the changes in the world since the pandemic swept from nation to nation, leaving death and fear in its wake.

"Oh, I forgot to tell you, Tom called and said he's taking us out to dinner tonight. It's a real blessing since I had no idea what I was planning to make. He said there was a new seafood restaurant he wants to try. Since you've come, we've been reading more about what things were like in your time. One of the things he found fascinating was going out for fish on Friday nights. We've always known there were seafood restaurants in the area, but we never thought of them for anything that wasn't a special occasion. Can you tell me why people went out for fish on a certain night each week?"

Caroline took a deep breath. "From what I remember it went back to the Catholic Church. Since the fish was a sign for Christianity, just after Jesus' time on earth, they felt that once a week and throughout Lent, their parishioners were expected to forego meat and eat fish instead. A friend of mine, who came from Wisconsin, told me of how almost every restaurant served a fish fry on Friday nights. It was literally unheard of in California, but I did accompany her to her favorite 'fish fry' restaurants. I enjoyed it, even though she said it wasn't as good as what she got when she was in Wisconsin."

"That explains it, I guess. Thank goodness the church here doesn't put such restrictions on us. I mean, belief in God is very important, but no one tells us what we can eat or do. Was your church that restrictive?"

"Not really. During Lent, we weren't expected to give anything up. It was more of a time for devotions and contemplation rather than one of withholding things. Easter was always such a joyous occasion. Between that and Christmas, those were the most festive times of the year. I am so pleased to see people today have gone back to worshiping God."

"Isn't it funny to see how things have evolved over the years. From what I've been told, there have been many false prophets saying the end of the world was at hand."

"I remember many of them. Of course, if the pandemic didn't wipe out the population of this planet, I can only believe it's all in God's hands. If it hadn't been, no one would have found me at that cryogenics lab. I go by what the Bible says, 'you know not the day nor the hour'."

"I guess that's a good way to look at things."

After checking the clock, Nora and Caroline went to get cleaned up to go out to dinner with Tom. As much as Caroline would have liked to have taken a nap, her discussion with Nora took more time than usual.

~ * ~

Although Caroline expected Tom to take them to an expensive seafood restaurant like the one she'd visited with her friend over a century earlier, she was surprised when they drove up to a very small establishment, with the name CULVER'S emblazoned across the front window.

For a moment, she had a memory surface that she hadn't thought about since awakening. "As I recall, just before all hell broke loose with the pandemic, a drive-in restaurant called Culver's was opened in our neighborhood in Los Angeles. They were famous for their butter burgers, frozen custard, and of course, for their fish fry. My friend said she wanted to try it because she remembered the restaurant from when she lived in Wisconsin. Of course, we never got a chance to go. After my husband died in China, I had no desire to go out. The rest we know is history. I was doing some research on the pandemic and looked up my friend. Unfortunately, I found that she died of the pandemic. Because of the state telling everyone to stay at home, she never even had a funeral. It was so sad to read about all the hardships this country, as well as others around the world, suffered because of that stupid virus. I was frozen just days before the lockdown occurred."

Tom nodded. "I've read all those horror stories, too. When I was talking to a coworker, I mentioned how you were talking about the fish fries of the past. That's when he mentioned this place. The story goes it was started in Wisconsin as a drive-in restaurant and they used only hand-breaded cod. Of course, the day of drive-in restaurants is long past, but they say the food here is excellent."

Caroline was intrigued. It was entirely possible tonight she could enjoy the same food her friend so highly recommended.

They stepped into the small storefront restaurant and Caroline was struck by how comfortable she was here. It was as if she was, once again, in the twenty-first century. The inside contained several small tables and booths, along with a counter where the customers could place their orders.

While Caroline felt right at home, she could tell Nora was disappointed at the informal atmosphere.

"Are you telling me I got dressed up to come to a place like this?" Nora complained.

"It's not what I expected either, but we have to give it a chance," Thomas replied. "Think of this as an adventure. Who knows we might be pleasantly surprised?"

Caroline didn't hesitate in ordering the two-piece cod dinner with a side of green beans rather than the offered French fries.

Nora and Tom followed her lead but opted for the French fries that came with the meal.

"I've noticed," Tom said, once their food was delivered, "you rarely eat potatoes. Why is that?"

"Back in the good old days, I had a problem with my weight. I realized that starches like potatoes, bread and rice turned to sugars and eventually unwanted weight. I was never a big fan of potatoes, so it wasn't much of a problem to give them up. It was the same with the bread. Now rice was something else. Since my husband was half Chinese, we ate a lot of Chinese/American food and the rice was a staple."

"I can't imagine anyone having a problem with their weight," Nora commented.

"I've wondered about that. I rarely see anyone who would be considered obese in the twenty-second century. Do you have any idea why that is?"

Tom thought for a moment. "I honestly don't know. When I was in college, I remember reading about the changes that were made in food after the pandemic. Somehow, the scientists derived an additive for food that decreased the fat and caloric content while retaining the flavor as well as the nutritional benefits. I guess that could be the answer to your question."

Caroline enjoyed the taste of the fish as well as the green beans and coleslaw that came with the dinner. While Tom and Nora sipped on their sodas, Caroline delighted in the taste of the ice tea that came as part of the meal.

"I have to admit," Nora said, "this is some of the best fish I've ever eaten. It's so different from the designer seafood restaurants we usually go to. I wouldn't mind coming back here again."

"I totally agree. How about I pop for dessert?" Caroline inquired. "I saw on the menu they have everything from cones to sundaes and even sodas."

"What are sodas?" Tom asked.

"That's something I remember as a kid growing up. They are made with ice cream, or in this case custard, with flavoring and soda water. I was always partial to the chocolate ones. As I remember, my mom liked the cherry ones and my grandma liked pineapple."

After looking over the menu board, Caroline ordered a chocolate soda, Tom a chocolate malt, and Nora a hot fudge sundae. Taking their sweet treats back to their table, they sampled each of the desserts.

"These are just like I remember them being. Right down to that hot fudge sundae you have, Nora. I am so glad you found this place. It could become my favorite guilty pleasure in this new world. Especially since I won't have to worry about gaining weight as long as I remember to do everything in moderation."

Tom laughed at her comment. "You never cease to amaze me. I don't know how well I would do if I went to sleep in one world and woke up in a completely alien society."

"What you tend to forget, my dear nephew, is that going to sleep was my choice. The library job has been godsend. I can do the research and relive the life I enjoyed before the world went crazy."

"I'll bet Aaron is another perk of your job," Nora teased.

Caroline broke into a wide grin. "I never thought I'd say this, but yes, Aaron is an important part of the job. He could become a wonderful addition in my life as well. Who would have thought that at the age of over a hundred years old, I could cultivate a special friend?"

Chapter Eight

Caroline was up earlier than Tom and Nora, giving her the chance to prepare one of her specialties, a baked omelet. After finishing her prep, she placed it into the oven and did the necessary clean up.

"What is that wonderful aroma?" Nora asked, when she came into the kitchen.

"Just a little something I enjoyed making on Saturday mornings. I learned how to make a baked omelet from my husband's mother. She was a chef and met his father when she applied to work at his Chinese/American restaurant. The rest, as they say, is history."

"I don't understand, the name Lewis doesn't sound Chinese to me," Nora said.

"It wasn't. His father had been adopted from China. Even though he was Chinese by birth, the family who adopted him were English missionaries by the name of Lewis. Therefore, even though they incorporated his Chinese name into his name, his last name became Lewis."

"That's all very interesting, but how long before we get to taste your culinary masterpiece?" Tom inquired.

Before she could answer, the doorbell rang, interrupting their conversation. While Caroline checked on the omelet, Tom answered the door.

"You're just in time, come in and join us for breakfast."

Caroline turned to see Aaron enter the kitchen.

"I didn't plan to impose on you for breakfast," Aaron greeted her. "My plan was to ask you to go out to breakfast with me and spend the day taking a road trip."

"What about our tickets for the theatre?"

"I got a message this morning that the theatre was having problems. A burst pipe or something, so our tickets will have to be used at a later date."

Caroline pretended to pout. "Since that's the case, I made enough breakfast for all of us, let me treat you for a change. All I have left to do is make the sauce for the omelet."

"I never asked, what is in your concoction?"

"It's actually called baked egg fu yung. It was my mother-in-law's creation. She developed it when she first started working at the restaurant. She felt uneasy using the original recipe, since the patties were fried in hot grease. In this version, you get all of the taste without the grease. It was an immediate hit with everyone at the restaurant. She would make it on demand in single serving sizes. For the family she prepared it in larger proportions. Now, grab a cup of coffee and scoot so I can finish everything up."

While Caroline busied herself at the stove, Nora set the table and the guys took their coffee into the living room.

"I've always enjoyed eating egg fu yung, but I have to admit whatever I've had in the past can't hold a candle to your version of it," Aaron said.

"I'm glad you like it. Can you give me an idea of where we're going on our outing?"

"I thought you might like to see where I grew up. My parents owned property in Wisconsin at Lake Geneva. Now it belongs to my sister and myself. We don't get up there as often as we'd like, but there's a caretaker who looks after the place for us. I called ahead and told the staff we'd be there for dinner tonight. I made reservations for four, hoping Tom and Nora would agree to join us. I also reserved three rooms so we can spend the night. What do you say, Tom, would you and Nora care to join us on our little adventure?"

Although Caroline would have preferred to be alone with Aaron for the afternoon and maybe even spend the night together, she said nothing.

"Lake Geneva?" Tom questioned. "You own property up there? That's one of the hottest tourist destinations in the Midwest. How do you maintain it?"

Aaron chuckled. "To be truthful, it doesn't cost me a thing. The resort is self-sufficient. The story goes that, after the pandemic as well as the destruction of the East and West coasts of our country, my great-grandfather invested in a property up there that was floundering, as was much of the country. The economy was shot to hell. Thank goodness my family managed their finances well and were able to purchase it for pennies on the dollar. Once the economy got back to normal, the property became a magnet for tourists with money to spend and with places like the East and West coast, along with Las Vegas, destroyed, they cashed in big. They were able to increase their holdings and open several casinos. My sister and I have good managers running everything. Throughout the years, we have been able to live off the interest from the investments. It's been perfect for both of us. She enjoys her life as a teacher and the extra money I receive makes the small salary the library pays me enough to live on."

Tom scratched his head. "Well, I'll be damned. As many times as we went out together in the past, I never suspected you had such wealth."

"You weren't supposed to. Our father instilled in us that no matter how much wealth the family had, the only thing that mattered was what we earned on our own merits. Now that you know, are you willing to accompany us?"

Once Tom and Nora agreed, the household became a hotbed of activity. With the kitchen cleaned up to the satisfaction of both Nora and Caroline, they took about fifteen minutes for each of them to pack an overnight bag.

The hovercraft that Aaron brought was much larger than the one he used on a daily basis. It would, indeed, hold all four of them in addition to their luggage comfortably.

~ * ~

The trip to Lake Geneva took less than half an hour. Traveling above the countryside of rural Illinois and Wisconsin gave Caroline a majestic view of the world as she never imagined it. In her former life, she grew up in Los Angeles and rarely saw life in the country. Even the trips she took with her husband to China were always to the larger cities where his relatives lived and worked.

"This is beautiful. Is Lake Geneva like this?" she inquired.

"Hardly," Aaron replied. "It's a bustling hotbed of activity, even in the winter. At this time of the year, people come not only for the gambling but for the activities associated with the lake. People like to go swimming as well as boating."

"What about water skiing?" Caroline asked, after searching her memory of the water sports enjoyed during the twentieth and twenty-first centuries.

"It's one of the reasons I made the decision to come up here when our plans for going to the theatre tonight were cancelled. This is a big weekend up here because of the water ski show. The local ski team puts one on every weekend, but today is special since there are several other teams coming for a competition. Thank goodness I was able to get rooms for tonight. I was afraid they would be sold out. Of course, I shouldn't have worried. There is always a three-bedroom suite that is reserved for either me or my sister. Since she and her husband are visiting their daughter in Missouri this weekend, I knew they wouldn't be using the suite."

Tom laughed at Aaron's statement. "I guess it pays to be the boss. I've always wanted to bring Nora up here, but the cost has been prohibitive."

"You won't have to worry about that this weekend, Tom. Everything is on me, or I should say, on the hotel. It's a perk that I don't take advantage of as often as I should. It was fun when my wife was alive. We'd come up about once a month, but once she was no longer with me, I wasn't about to come alone. I considered coming up alone with Caroline but I decided for our first date she might be more comfortable having you and Nora with us."

Although Caroline wished she was here alone with Aaron, she knew she would enjoy sharing the experience with Tom and Nora.

Once Aaron secured his hovercraft in the area designated for docking, they were met by an employee of the resort driving something that resembled a golf cart like the ones she used in the twenty-first century.

"These carts are unique," Nora observed. "How are they run?"

"The same as the hovercraft. They use solar energy. I am told when my ancestors first purchased this place they were run on electricity."

Caroline watched as the driver loaded their overnight bags into the back of the cart. With everything secured, they sat on the seats and allowed the driver to take them from the docking area to the main hotel.

Her first impression of this facility was the sound of slot machines. If she closed her eyes, she could pretend she was back in Las Vegas with her husband when they enjoyed the bounty the city had to offer on many occasions.

"It's so good to have you staying with us again, Mr. Phillips," the desk clerk greeted them. "Your suite is ready for you. I'm told you are interested in the water ski show. The next round of competition is due to begin at two. You and your party will have time to enjoy the luncheon that is being served in the dining room."

Aaron thanked the man and gave him a generous tip. "Our bags will be taken to the suite. Since we don't have to bother with that, let's go in and have some lunch before the competition begins again." He went on to explain that the resort was all-inclusive, so the meals were included in the price of the rooms.

Once in the dining room, they were greeted with a fantastic buffet containing everything anyone could want in the way of salads and sandwiches. After building her salad, Caroline took a bowl of mixed fruit to complete her lunch selection.

If any of the diners recognized Aaron, no one mentioned the fact they were in the company of the owner of the resort. As soon as they finished eating, they went out to the viewing area by the lake in order to watch the competition.

Since Aaron had dressed casually, Caroline, Tom and Nora followed his lead. The day was turning out to be warm, so Caroline was glad she'd chosen shorts and a comfortable top to wear.

Each of the ski teams performed their routines with only one or two mishaps. They all agreed it would be hard for the judges to declare a winner based on their abilities, which seemed to be equally distributed between all of the teams.

With the competition completed and the festivities winding down, they went up to the suite for a short nap before going down for dinner. Aaron told them he'd checked the menu and tonight was surf and turf. The surf for tonight was shrimp and the turf was prime rib.

"Did you grow up living at the resort?" Tom asked, as they waited for their dinner to be brought to their table.

"My grandparents lived in the suite, but my parents bought a small cottage on the other side of the lake. I alternated between staying at the resort and living in the cottage. When I went away to college and met my wife, we decided coming up here was a special getaway. My wife was a corporate attorney and I've always enjoyed my job at the library. When the resort was left to my sister and myself, we both were already well into our careers. It made more sense to leave the day-to-day running of the resort to the experts and reap the benefits."

"What about the cottage? Do you still own it?" Nora asked.

"We do, but now the manager of the resort lives there. It's one of the perks of the job. We don't charge him rent and he takes care of the upkeep as well as the household expenses. It works out well for all of us."

Caroline saw a man approaching their table. The way he carried himself, she decided he must be the manager Aaron was talking about.

"Aaron, it's good to see you. It's been too long since you've come up here to visit."

Aaron got to his feet and shook the man's hand. "It's good to see you, too, Walt. I was just telling my friends about you. I'd like you to meet Tom and Nora Jamison and Caroline Lewis."

Walt held out his hand in greeting, then turned his full attention to

Caroline. "I'm honored to have you staying with us, Ms. Lewis. I read all about your awakening on the internet. How are you liking the twenty-second century?"

"There are a lot of new things to get used to. I was surprised when Aaron told us about this place. The casino reminds me of the times my husband and I went to Las Vegas. The grounds as well as the food are like nothing I've ever experienced before."

They exchanged more pleasantries until their dinners were served and Walt moved on to other tables.

"It looks like you and Walt are old friends," Tom observed.

"We are. We went to school together. While I studied library science, he majored in hotel management. When we were in need of a manager, I had no reservations about offering him the position."

"Didn't your parents or grandparents object to you hiring someone?" Nora asked.

"My grandparents passed on before I went away to college and by the time I graduated, my parents were ready to retire. They were very happy with my hiring Walt, since they knew him as well as I did. The folks come to visit at Christmas, but otherwise, they are very happy with their retirement in Arkansas. Whatever decisions my sister and I make are perfectly fine with them."

~ * ~

On Sunday, Aaron insisted they accompany him to the church he'd grown up attending, before they watched the last of the ski competition and returned to the city.

Caroline enjoyed watching the skiers perform their routines and was excited when the team she'd picked was declared the winners.

Even though she knew they had to return to everyday life, she wished they could have stayed longer. She loved the serenity of the resort on the lake, even though the casino didn't attract her. Had this been a hundred years ago, she would have dropped a lot of money at one of the casinos Adam enjoyed visiting, but she now realized her gambling days were over. She gambled when she opted to spend twenty thousand dollars to be frozen at the cryogenics lab and won. In the future, no other gamble would ever pay off as well as the last one she'd made in 2020.

The flight back to the city didn't last long enough to suit Caroline. She wanted to spend more time alone with Aaron. Perhaps their next date would be without Tom and Nora.

"I hope the two of you don't mind if Caroline and I drop you off. I'd like to take her out to dinner," Adam suggested.

"Of course, we don't," Tom replied. "As much as we've enjoyed this weekend, we thought the two of you would have liked a little more alone time. To be truthful, I was planning on taking my wife someplace special for dinner tonight, just the two of us, if you get my drift."

Caroline knew Tom had no such plans, but was making Aaron feel better about his desire for them to be alone.

Once they let Tom and Nora off, Aaron turned toward one of the far western suburbs of the city. Within a few minutes, he landed in front of a small family type restaurant.

"This is a delightful place," Caroline said, as she looked over the menu. "My mouth is watering over the German chicken."

Aaron turned his attention to the menu. "Hmm…I don't think that's anything I would order. I'm more of a liver and onions man myself. I've never been a fan of sauerkraut."

She smiled. This was something she would have heard Adam saying. Her German background meant she was brought up on eating many things his Chinese/American pallet wouldn't accept. It was the same with the liver and onions Aaron insisted on ordering. It certainly was nothing she would have ever ordered.

"I'm beginning to think although we do share some tastes, in others we are very different," Aaron said, as he raised his water glass in a toast.

"Difference is good, but I hope we aren't so entirely different we cannot make some important decisions together."

"What kind of decisions are you talking about?"

Caroline thought for a moment before answering. "I would like to go shopping next weekend for a small house or maybe a condo. I've been happy staying with Tom and Nora, but I feel it's time I find a place of my own."

Aaron frowned at her comment. "I can understand your motivation, but moving out of their house would mean you'd no longer be within walking distance of the library. Are you ready to learn how to pilot your own hovercraft?"

"Oh, good heavens no. I have told you I have no worries about money. For what it would cost me to own a hovercraft, to say nothing about maintaining it, I can afford to use public transportation whenever I need to. As for how I would get to the library, I'm hoping to find something in the same neighborhood as Tom and Nora's home. I've seen some complexes in the area. I honestly don't know what anything is worth. What I would have paid in 2020 might not be what places are nowadays."

"Nowadays?" Aaron questioned. "I've read that word in many of the old books in the library, but I've never heard anyone say it."

"You have to remember, I come from a different time and place. Will you agree to come with me next weekend?"

"I would be honored. It's possible if we get an early start on Saturday, we can still use our tickets for the seven o'clock performance of *Hamilton*."

Caroline hoped things would go as smoothly as Aaron predicted, but she had her doubts. She recalled purchasing the home she shared with Adam in Los Angeles. They looked for the perfect property for over six months before making the decision of where to settle.

Chapter Nine

Caroline found she was busier than usual at work. Enough so she didn't have time to research the real estate listings for Tom and Nora's neighborhood.

Aaron, on the other hand, had become a permanent fixture in her daily activities. He was usually in his office when she arrived for work and came to her office at precisely noon to take her to the cafeteria for lunch.

"Have you checked the real estate listings?" he asked, once they were seated at their usual table.

"To be truthful, I haven't had a chance to even look at them. It's amazing the amount of people who have been contacting me to do research for them. A lot of it is looking into people's family trees. The most interesting one was someone who wanted to know about their great-grandmother. It turned out the woman they were looking for was my best friend. It's hard to realize the woman who played such an important part in my life is now considered part of ancient history."

"I'm certain much of your research ends like that. It must be hard to research the late twentieth and early twenty-first centuries and realize you lived through those times that are now part of history.

"Changing the subject, I have taken the time to look into available properties. There is a new condo complex about three blocks east of here. They do have some units for sale, but I have no idea what your budget is."

For a moment, Caroline didn't quite know what to say. What if prices were so exorbitant that she couldn't afford to buy something.

"I honestly don't know what prices are."

Aaron laughed. "This coming from the person everyone calls the Queen of Research. If this had been 2020, what do you think you would have paid for a condo?"

"Adam and I bought a large house in the 1990s for four hundred thousand dollars. By 2020, I could have purchased a two-bedroom condo for that much. With those numbers running around in my head, I have a feeling I could be looking at a million or possibly more."

"It's a good thing I found the time to research for you. Before the pandemic, real estate costs in California skyrocketed. When the natural disasters struck both coasts, the bottom fell out of everything. Tom and I were talking about it last weekend and he said your brother was lucky to have been able to sell your place, as well as his, before the disaster struck. He must have had a premonition of what was to come, since he relocated to the Chicago area two years before everything on the west coast was destroyed."

Caroline could hardly believe what Aaron was telling her. "My brother was the CEO of a large medical marijuana company in the Los Angeles area. I never thought he would have moved the operation here, but as I think of it, Illinois had just passed a law legalizing marijuana. It makes sense that he would have moved his operation here. I know he wanted both of us to be closer to our family here in the Midwest. I wasn't so sure about the move at the time. I guess his ideas were the best in the long run."

"Your family still owns the marijuana operation and it's revolutionized the medical community. In reality, Tom would never have to work another day in his life, but he has a love for the law and is the corporate attorney for the company."

She nodded. She knew about Tom's law practice, but had no idea one of his clients was the company her brother headed up back in the twenty-first century.

"Getting back to the cost of things, these new condos that are for sale are running from between one hundred and eighty to two hundred thousand dollars. They look quite nice, on paper that is. I haven't actually seen them. If all else fails, I have a guest cottage that would be perfect for you. The only drawback would be I'd be your landlord and you wouldn't own the place."

Caroline contemplated Aaron's offer. It would be nice to live close to him, but at this time in her life she wanted to at least have a taste of independence.

"Do we have to make an appointment to see those condos?"

"I'm way ahead of you. I made an appointment with the real estate agent handling the condos for nine tomorrow morning. That isn't too early for you, is it? I mean that would give us plenty of time to at least look at what they have to offer and still be in the city in time for dinner and the theatre."

"I think that will be perfect."

~ * ~

Although Tom tried to talk Caroline out of looking at the condo, she decided not to be dissuaded.

"I told you when I first arrived that I wanted my own place. It's not like I'm looking at a place a million miles away. I looked this place up and it's less than a mile from here. Besides, I haven't bought the place, I'm just looking at it. Who knows? I might not like it. If I don't, I can always rent Aaron's guest house."

"You might what?" Tom bellowed. "I know the two of you are attracted to one another and that's a good thing. I mean, Aaron is a great guy, but don't you think that living in his guest house is a bit much? What would people say?"

Caroline shook her head. Before she could formulate a response, the doorbell rang. "Ah, that must be Aaron. If nothing else, he's punctual."

"Are you ready for our appointment?" Aaron asked, when he entered the kitchen.

"I certainly am. I did look the condo up on the internet last night and it does look like something I would be interested in. I'll let you know what I decide."

Nora winked at her broadly and wished her well in her adventure for the morning.

~ * ~

Caroline toured two of the condos. One was on the fifteenth floor, while the other was within a quad sitting with a backyard.

"What do you think?" Aaron asked when they finished the tour.

"I liked the one in the high rise, if for no other reason than the security, but it's just not me. I think I'd like to put an offer in on the unit in the quad. When Adam and I were married, I always wanted to be able to putter around in the garden, but we were so involved in the business, there was never any time. We hired someone to do the work, but it wasn't the same."

"I never figured you for a gardener, but I do think this place is perfect for you."

By noon, Caroline had put in a cash offer and now only had to wait for it to be accepted. After a light lunch, Aaron dropped her off at Tom's home to get ready for their trip into the city.

"Did you find something?" Nora asked.

"I most certainly did. I put an offer in on a unit within a quad. It's just perfect for me and there's even a yard and small garden where I can putter around next summer."

"Are you sure about this?" Tom inquired. "Did you look into the condo fees? Wasn't it outrageously expensive?"

"I know you're looking out for my best interest, but the price was less than I expected it to be and the condo fees are also manageable. I don't think I could rent an apartment for the cost of the fees. I can pay cash for the place. It also has all-new appliances and even though I don't have to mow the lawn, I'll be able to plant some flowers. It's enough for me. I do hope you will be willing to help me shop for the furnishing and to give me tips on how to decorate the place."

"You know we will," Nora assured her. "How long before you can start shopping for what you need?"

"I'm hoping to hear back from the seller next week to see if they are willing to accept my offer. Once they do, I guess I can move in whenever I want."

Caroline looked to Tom. His expression was one she couldn't read. "I hope you're not upset with me getting a place of my own."

"I'm not displeased, but I hope you're making the right choice. I'd hate to see you get burned by purchasing something so quickly."

"Oh, Tom, you're being overprotective. I agree with Caroline, she needs to have her own space and she can't do it here with us. I don't want to see her leave, but I'm excited to think she's found a place where she'll be comfortable."

"Comfortable," Tom countered, "but will she be safe? The way it sounds, it's not a high security building like one of those high-rise condos."

"No, it isn't, but it's in a gated community," Caroline said. "As I recall, from the good old days, those communities were perfectly safe. I know what I'm doing and you know it, too. This life is all new to me, but I'm positive this will all work out for the best. Just think, I'll be able to host you and Nora for dinner parties. Who knows, I might make some new friends within the quad. I'm so excited about this."

Nora came to Caroline's side. "You know we're only concerned with your happiness. I'm thrilled to think about you getting your own place. I can hardly wait until we can start looking for all the furnishings for your new home."

~ * ~

Caroline put the finishing touches to her makeup and made one last check of her hair, when the doorbell rang. From the living room, she could hear Tom greeting Aaron.

"What do you think of this crazy move Caroline is making?" Tom inquired.

"I think it's great. The condo she looked at today is perfect for her.

Of course, I would have liked to have her living in my guest house, but she's far too independent to be interested in renting it."

"I heard about your guest house."

Tom's voice sounded annoyed.

"Caroline mentioned it earlier. I'd forgotten you even had that place before that. Are you saying you're encouraging her to move in with you? Don't you think it's a little too early in your relationship for something like that?"

"For your information, when we bought the house, it was because of the guest house. It was for my mother-in-law. Unfortunately, both my wife and her mother were killed in that hovercraft accident. The house has sat vacant ever since. I've held onto the house as well as the guest house ever since, hoping someday to find a renter. After seeing those condos with Caroline today, I decided it's time for me to make a change in my life, too. Once I got home, I put in an offer on the condo she didn't want. Unlike Caroline, I've had enough of yard work and gardening. The unit in the high rise is perfect for me. Next week, I'll be putting my house on the market. To be truthful, Caroline has breathed new life into me for the first time in years. Change is good, not only for her but also for me."

"Did I hear you correctly?" Caroline asked as she entered the living room. "Are you actually interested in that other condo?"

"I am. It's time I downsize. The fact it's close to the library is a plus."

"What about your hovercrafts?"

"I'm trying to decide which one of them to keep. I'm leaning toward the larger one, in case I decide to take people with me. I usually only use the smaller one for commuting back and forth to work. Considering I would be within walking distance, it would no longer be necessary. Of course, if you want to learn how to pilot one, I would be willing to sell it to you."

"Oh no, not me. I only drove in Los Angeles because it was a necessity, especially after Adam died. I know it was only a few days, but that was enough for me. The traffic was horrendous and I hated every minute of it. I'm content with walking to wherever I need to go or using public transportation."

The two men both had horrified looks on their faces. "What about grocery shopping?" Tom questioned.

"I've read enough about the effects of the pandemic to know that many stores became adept at taking online orders and delivering them to people's homes. I don't think I will starve. I also won't need to learn how to fly one of those hovercrafts. Being a passenger is just fine with me. Even in inclement weather, I'm certain I can hire a cab, or an Uber."

"What's an Uber?" Aaron wanted to know.

His question shocked Caroline. She went on to explain about the private people who used their personal cars to take people wherever they wanted to go in the early twenty-first century.

"I see. Nowadays we call them Lifts."

The discussion could have gone on for hours, but Aaron reminded Caroline they had to leave for the city in order to enjoy a leisurely dinner before they went to the theatre.

~ * ~

It didn't take long for them to fly from the suburbs to downtown Chicago. Once they landed and had their craft secured, they took a leisurely walk to the restaurant located close to the theatre.

While Caroline took in the changed landscape of downtown Chicago, she stopped in her tracks when she saw a familiar landmark.

"Oh, look, there's 'The Bean'," she said, pointing to the sculpture in the middle of what was once considered one of the "must see" attractions in Chicago.

"The what?" Aaron questioned, a look of bewilderment on his face.

"The Bean. It was commissioned in 2004 and completed in 2006. When Adam and I came to Chicago for a family reunion in 2014, we made this one of the things we visited. If I was able to access the pictures we took while we were here, you could see Adam and me standing in front of it. There were so many people here that day, all taking pictures. It was warm enough that the little kids were wading in the reflective pool. It was a wonderful day. We even stopped at a sandwich shop and bought sandwiches, chips and sodas to bring back and enjoy the warmth of the day. It's made of highly polished steel and at the time it was dedicated, it was touted as appearing to be seamless and reflective."

"That's so strange," Aaron commented. "I've seen this hundreds of times but never knew what it meant or why it was in this park. Did you say there was a reflective pool? I don't ever remember seeing one here before."

Caroline tried hard to keep her emotions in check. Aaron's bewilderment came as a surprise. How could he work in the research department of a Chicago area library and not know about 'The Bean'?

"I have a feeling the pandemic changed a lot of things for the people in our country, including the appreciation of works of art. It's so sad to think that the city hasn't kept the memory of this landmark alive and well for future generations."

Aaron took her hand and brought it to his lips. "I think it's time I take a closer look at this piece of art or this landmark as you call it. It is unique."

Caroline smiled as they walked toward the looming sculpture. She glanced to where she remembered the reflecting pool and was disappointed to see it had been removed and the area filled in with grass. In her mind's eye she could see the large pillars at each end of the pool that projected a variety of holograms. Looking across the expanse of grass, she realized the only thing that remained as she remembered was "The Bean."

"It's so sad to think that something that was so special has been neglected and virtually forgotten. It makes me wonder whether other parks and sculptures have also been decimated."

"I think that is something best for you to research at the library. For now, let's get to the restaurant and enjoy our meal before we go to the theatre."

Sadly, Caroline understood what Aaron meant. She knew once she researched what happened after the pandemic, she would find that places she'd visited with Adam were, more than likely, lost to the world of the twenty-second century.

Chapter Ten

Monday morning, Caroline was still reliving the performance of *Hamilton* they saw on Saturday night. She knew she should be researching the national landmarks on the east and west coasts of the United States, but decided to put off doing it. Instead, she reveled in the memory of the day they'd spent together over the weekend.

All in all, Saturday had been a completely delightful day. The two condos they'd seen were both not only new but also exactly where she was looking to live. She wanted to be in a community and both places offered that. Even with the condo fees, she was confident with her choice of the unit within the quad setting.

Thinking about the high-rise unit, she smiled to herself at the prospect of Aaron living so close to her. It came as a pleasant surprise when Aaron expressed an interest in purchasing it. In her wildest dreams she would have never thought her life in the future could have turned out in this way.

A knock at her office door brought Caroline out of her contemplations.

"Enter," she called. It didn't come as a surprise when Aaron entered her office.

"Are you having problems with your communicator today?" he asked.

"Not that I know of, why?"

"I just had a call from the realtor representing the Condo Association. They've been trying to reach you all morning."

Caroline glanced at her wrist. How could she have forgotten to put on her communicator after her shower this morning?

"I-I must have left it at home this morning. I was running late and..."

"Not to worry," Aaron interrupted. "I talked to them and assured them you were waiting for their call. You can contact them on my communicator."

In her excitement over the call from the realtor, she didn't ask if Aaron's offer had been accepted.

"This is Caroline Lewis. My friend tells me you have been trying to reach me," she said as soon as the connection was made.

"Yes, we have. We have been in contact with the Condo Association and they have accepted your offer. We understand you work through the week, so they have agreed to have the closing on Saturday morning at ten. Will that work for you?"

"Oh, yes, it will work. Thank you so much for your call."

"It looks like both of us will be meeting with the Condo Association on Saturday," Aaron said, once the communicator screen went black. "When they called, they assured me both of our offers were accepted. My closing is also set for Saturday morning. Now all I have to do is either rent or sell my property."

"Oh, Aaron, I can't believe the two of us will both be living in that complex. I was praying we would be accepted. That said, I've been thinking about the conversation you had with Tom the other night about your second vehicle. Since my unit comes with a docking station. I can see no reason why you can't keep both of your vehicles and park one in my unit."

Aaron pulled Caroline to her feet and embraced her warmly. "You were thinking ahead. We should have a celebratory dinner. Where would you like to go tonight?"

"Not tonight. I don't want to jinx anything. Let's make plans for Saturday night. I'm certain I still remember how to cook. As my only family in the area, I'd like to include Tom and Nora in our celebration."

"I was hoping for something a little more private, but your wish is my command, my lady."

She laughed at how old-fashioned his response would have sounded even a hundred years ago. "Something tells me you've been reading too many classics. Even so, I love your chivalry. It's very cavalier. Perhaps a private celebration could be arranged as well as the one I have in mind. I still remember many of the recipes I used throughout my marriage to Adam."

"You don't have to convince me. I tasted your baked egg fu yung and it was delicious. I am looking forward to whatever culinary delights you have in mind for our celebration with Tom and Nora. Would you accompany me to our own private celebration tomorrow night at a lovely little steak restaurant I know of not far from here?"

"I would be honored."

Aaron kissed her hand before leaving her office. With the call from the realtor representing the condo association, her mind was put at ease about her future.

Turning back to her computer, she put in a search for many of the parks and national monuments she and Adam visited over a hundred years earlier.

~ * ~

By the time she was ready to go home, she'd shed many tears over the national treasurers that had been lost because of the natural disasters. How had Johnathan known to leave California before any of this occurred?

She pondered the question she'd posed to herself all afternoon. By the time she got home, she was more than ready to see if Tom could give her an answer.

"How much do you know about why my brother moved to Chicago?" she asked over dinner.

"The story I've always heard was that, when you disappeared, he decided he wanted to move here to be close to the rest of your family. There had been predictions of pending disasters hitting the west coast for many years and finally in 2025, he made the decision to make the move.

The disasters struck in 2027. The entire country was devastated over the loss of the cities and monuments on both coasts. The entire family was thrilled by the thought that my Great Grandparents were safe here in the Midwest."

Caroline nodded. Unlike she had thought, there had been warnings, but how many people heeded them? All the time she spent on the West Coast she'd heard about the big earthquake that would someday hit and decimate the state of California. At the time she hadn't given it much thought. There were earthquakes, but everyone was used to them and decided to go with the flow.

"I did some research on what happened on the West Coast today and I was devastated by it. You said the same thing happened on the East Coast. Does that mean Washington, D.C. is no longer our capital?"

"I've thought a lot about that," Tom replied. "The history books I read in school said it was a miracle that Washington, D.C. was spared the fate of most of the East Coast. Once the aliens made their presence known, they told us it was by divine design that the city had been spared. They told us they had been monitoring our planet and especially the United States for many years. It made sense because of all of the stories we've heard over the years about extraterrestrials appearing throughout history. Of course, that's not to say New York was spared because it wasn't. The financial capital of the United States is now in St. Louis which makes more sense since it's closer to the geographical center of the country."

Caroline nodded. All of this information was inconceivable to her. How could the most prosperous country on earth have suffered so many disasters and still survived?

It was Nora who changed the subject. "Did you hear from the realtor for Condo Association today?"

"Yes, I did. No thanks to me, though. I forgot to put on my communicator this morning and they had to contact Aaron to reach me."

"Oh dear, I didn't realize you didn't have it with you," Nora lamented.

"Everything worked out for the best," Caroline assured them. "They called Aaron to tell him the offer he put in had been accepted.

While they were talking to him, they mentioned getting in touch with me. He came to my office and we contacted them on his communicator. I am happy to let you know I'm closing on my unit on Saturday morning and Aaron is also closing at the same time. It looks like I'm going to be out of your hair sooner rather than later."

"You know we don't want you to leave, but I can understand you wanting your privacy. Do you mind if I go with you to the closing? You know, as your legal advisor."

"That would be good. I'm planning to have a celebration of the closing on Saturday night, here at your house. I've been putting together a menu in my head all afternoon. Of course, you and Nora are invited. Once we have the closing, we can go over to the unit so Nora and I can make some plans for how to decorate and what I will be needing in the line of furnishings."

Caroline relaxed after they began talking about her new condo. The realization of what occurred after she made the decision to be put into suspended animation at the cryogenics lab suddenly seemed to be too much to handle. For a while, she needed to think about the future rather than the past.

Tuesday morning, Caroline chose a dress she knew Aaron had never seen her wear before. Since they were going out to celebrate their new living arrangements, she wanted to look her very best. The last thing she did was to make certain to attach her communicator to her left wrist.

As soon as she stepped out onto the porch, she realized the weather was changing. Summer was coming to an end and autumn was making its presence known. With a chill in the air, she went back into the house to get a light jacket.

When she got to the library, she decided to do more checking into what Tom had been saying the previous evening at supper.

When she typed in "Alien Arrival On Earth" into the computer, a multitude of articles popped up on her screen. By noon, she'd read several of the suggested articles.

She was surprised to learn how the extraterrestrials made their presence known just prior to the disasters that happened on both the east and west coast of the United States. They had warned of the disasters. When they did, they helped the country recover from not only the physical damage but also to find a cure for the pandemic that preceded what might have completely destroyed every country in the world.

"Why haven't I heard of this before?" she asked Aaron when they met in the cafeteria for lunch.

"I guess it wasn't all that important. I've grown up knowing about the aliens who came to this planet to help humanity. It's part of history. I never considered what it was like before their arrival."

Caroline thought long and hard about what Aaron told her. "Are there aliens among us here in Chicago?"

"Not as many as there used to be. Once the financial hub was moved from New York to St. Louis, they established a colony in that area. They also have a colony in Virginia, not far from Washington, D.C., as well as a research center in Colorado."

She gasped. "Are they running the financial institutions and the government?"

"Not in the way you think. They are advisors to the government but also to the financial and medical communities. With their guidance, we have made great strides in finding cures for what were once incurable diseases. I doubt you will ever encounter one of them, but if you do, you would not know it. They are no different from the humans who have lived on this earth since the beginning of time. If you want to meet them, we could plan a trip to the St. Louis colony next summer."

~ * ~

After lunch, Caroline returned to her office. With few requests for information, she had time to think about what Aaron told her about the aliens who helped the United States and the world to recover from the natural disasters.

She remembered hearing stories about the crashing of a flying saucer in Roswell, New Mexico in the 1940s as well as those of the Greys. As a child, she'd often been frightened about being abducted by or even encountering one of the dreaded aliens. How could the stories that frightened her so much have come true with the visitors being so beneficial to mankind?

With nothing else to research, she typed "ALIEN" in the search bar. It came as no surprise when several websites appeared on the screen. Unsure of which one to check out first, she started at the top and worked her way down.

The amount of information she received was mind boggling. By the time she was ready to leave for the day, she learned of the strides made in the medical field because of the knowledge brought by the aliens. Also, the national debt had been eliminated with the discovery of new natural resources that brought more revenue to the country.

Another site proclaimed the return of the government of the people, by the people, and for the people. The traditional political parties were no longer in existence, having been replaced by men and women who no longer had political connections, but ran the government doing what was best for the people of the nation.

"It's a shame there had to be disasters to bring about what should have been done before the turn of the century," she confided to Aaron later as they ordered their dinner.

"I don't see things the same way as you do. The government has always functioned the way it does now. At least for as long as I can remember."

"Believe me, things were much different in 2020. The two main parties were the Republicans and the Democrats. If one party was in control of the government, the other party could never get their projects through either the Congress or the Senate. It was us against them, no matter what was going on. When I went to sleep, I worried about war with North Korea, the virus, global warming, and a myriad of other things that were going on. The president was calling the people of the opposing party liars and criminals, without anything to substantiate the claims. It had gotten so bad, I refused to even watch the nightly news."

Aaron had tears in his eyes as he listened to what she was telling him. "That's not the way things were taught while I was in history class. We were told that the form of government in the U.S. wasn't working but the aliens showed us a better way. It's been working for us ever since. I certainly didn't know about any corruption. It's a godsend that you have been able to come back to life and set all of the records straight."

"I agree, but as a woman, who would listen to me other than you? Perhaps it's best that the past stay buried. As far as I'm concerned, it was a dark time in our history that is probably best forgotten. Besides, this is supposed to be a celebration about our new homes. I much prefer talking about our future rather than the past. At least that's something we can control."

Aaron's mood lightened. "You're right. Our future does look bright and we have every right to celebrate."

He raised his water glass in a salute to her. Smiling, she raised her glass and touched his. If this had been while she and Adam were married, they would be drinking champagne, but under the laws of the land, alcoholic beverages were no longer served in restaurants. Once they moved into their new condos, she would make it a point to purchase a bottle of champagne for a proper toast in the privacy of their own homes.

Chapter Eleven

On Saturday morning Caroline and Nora left early to shop for what was needed for the evening celebration Caroline had been planning throughout the week. After they put away the groceries they'd purchased, they left for the office where they would be signing the papers to make her a proud home owner.

"I don't like the idea of you living alone," Tom said, as they made their way toward the realty office.

"There is no need to worry. This is a very safe neighborhood. If you're concerned about me getting lonely, I'm within walking distance of your house. I have a communicator and if I need anything, I can contact you. If the truth be known, I'm looking forward to cooking in my own kitchen and I'm sure Nora feels the same way. Two cooks in the same kitchen tend to get in each other's way. My mother used to say that house guests and fish all begin to stink after too many days."

Nora laughed at her comment. "I never heard that one before but it makes sense. It's not like I want you to leave, but I know you value your privacy."

Once they arrived at the docking station for the realty office, Caroline felt her heart skip a beat. For the first time in her life she was purchasing a home of her own. Her home in Los Angeles had been one Adam chose, even though he asked her opinion on it, she knew it probably wouldn't have been her choice. She would have much preferred a small cottage to the sprawling mansion Adam insisted on purchasing for them. The small condo was much more her idea of the ideal home.

The realtor gave her the papers to read over. The sheaf of papers was thick and for the first time she was pleased to have Tom there to give her the thumbnail sketch of what was being said.

When she toured the condo, she commented on how much she liked the window treatments. In the contracts she was now signing, it was spelled out in order to keep continuity throughout the community there would be no changes made to the window treatments. Every five years, the condo association would meet with the tenants and make the decision about what the new treatments would be.

Also, what came with her unit were all of the appliances: stove, refrigerator, dishwasher, microwave, washer and dryer, and they were the responsibility of the association, rather than the homeowner.

"Does everything meet with your approval, Ms. Lewis?" the realtor asked.

Caroline looked to Tom, who nodded his approval.

"Yes, I don't see anything I can't abide by. I do have the information for my bank to transfer the money to your account from mine."

"Are you planning to finance this through your bank?"

Caroline smiled. "No, this will be a cash sale. That meets with your approval, doesn't it?"

"Of course, it does."

She knew she was paving the way for Aaron to close on his property, as he was planning to also have a cash sale. She was pleased to think his wealth mirrored her own. That being the fact, she didn't have to think about either of them desiring the company of the other because of their money. In the twenty-first century, whether it was a man or a woman, they would be called a "gold digger."

After she signed the papers and arranged for the financial transfer of funds, Caroline relaxed. She watched as Aaron went through the same process to obtain his property. She marveled at the ease with which he handled the situation.

Her mind wandered back to her life with Adam. He told her that, as the man, he had more ability to handle financial situations. At the time, she had acquiesced to his wishes. Since his death, she decided to be more independent, whether or not she was making the right decision.

It was noon when they finally finished and Tom insisted on taking them out to lunch before the girls went home to begin creating the feast Caroline planned for the evening.

~ * ~

The events of the morning pumped Caroline with adrenaline. After arriving back at Tom's home, she began preparations for the evening meal. With everything under control, she joined Nora at the computer to order furnishings for her new home.

While she and Nora were occupied, Tom and Aaron talked about the prospect of the two of them living in the same complex.

Caroline caught bits and snatches of their conversation and realized Tom was worried about the propriety of the relationship she shared with Aaron. Hearing his concerns, she was more than ready to move into her own place. It was best if Tom and Nora didn't know of her every move. Even though chronologically she was a hundred and forty-two years old, mentally and physically she was no different from the woman who had made the decision to be put into suspended animation a hundred years ago. She had the same feelings and needs of the young woman she'd been when she lost Adam. She needed the companionship of a member of the opposite sex and if love happened, so be it.

~ * ~

On Sunday, after attending church, Caroline and Aaron went to his present home to decide which furnishings would look the best in his new condo.

She was amazed at the size of the home where he and his first wife lived together. The furnishings were ones she knew had been chosen with a woman's eye for decorating. The guest cottage, on the other hand, looked more like something Aaron would have chosen.

"I think the furnishings of the guest house would be more

appropriate for your new place," Caroline commented.

"I was thinking along those lines myself. I do think I'd like to get new bedroom furniture. What site did you use when you purchased your things?"

Caroline opened the page for the place where she'd bought the furniture she'd found. Together they looked through everything they had to offer before he found exactly what he was looking for.

It took a minimum of time before they arranged for the new furniture, along with what he was bringing from the guest house, to be delivered to their condos on the following Saturday.

"Have you looked into selling this place?" she asked.

"I have and I put it on the market as soon as I knew I'd been approved for the condo. I thought about renting it out, but decided I didn't want to be a landlord. My realtor is certain she has a buyer who would like to purchase both properties as a package deal. I'm just waiting for the logistics to be worked out."

~ * ~

Two weeks later, they were both settled in their new community. Aaron's properties sold quickly and the realtor even made arrangements to have the furnishings of the big house, as well as those he didn't want from the guest house, to be sold at an auction house in the city.

With autumn upon them and winter fast approaching, Aaron insisted on taking Caroline to the library on a daily basis. Even on days when she could have easily made the walk, she appreciated the warmth of his hovercraft.

Her life fell into a comfortable routine. On Tuesday, Wednesday and Friday, Aaron would leave her off at the library while he went to one of the outlying branches to oversee their various programs.

It was almost noon on a Tuesday morning when a knock at her office door turned her attention from the computer screen to whoever wanted her attention in person. To her surprise, a striking couple stood just outside her office door.

"How can I help you?" she asked, as she got to her feet to be on the same level as her visitors.

She immediately realized both the man and woman stood at least a foot taller than herself.

"Are you Caroline Lewis?" the woman inquired.

"Yes, I am. I'm afraid you have me at a disadvantage, since I don't think I've had the pleasure of meeting you before."

"I'd be surprised if you did know us," the man said, taking advantage of Caroline's welcoming gesture and entered the office. "My name is Cassion and my companion is Hodia. We represent the Council of Intergalactic Affairs."

Caroline's heart began to race. These people were the aliens she'd been researching for the past several weeks. Only yesterday she'd come across the website for the Council of Intergalactic Affairs. Could this be why these people were standing in her office?

"Again, I ask, how can I help you?"

Hodia held out her hand to Caroline. "We don't mean to alarm you. We know of you from the news reports we have been seeing about your miraculous return to life from suspended animation. Our people have also participated in this and we are anxious to ask you some questions about your experience. We would also appreciate it if you would agree to accompany us back to our medical facility in Denver, Colorado."

"D-Denver? I don't know what to say. I have obligations here at the library as well as to my family. Can't you get the information you need from the various tests that were run when I was first discovered in the facility in California? Why would I need to go to Denver to have all the same tests run for a second time?"

"Unfortunately, our doctors and researchers would like to do many tests the doctors you saw earlier are unaware of. Yours is a very unique situation. We know the effects of suspended animation on healthy individuals, but the fact you had cancer as well as other conditions makes your awakening an extraordinary occurrence. On the planet from where we have come, you would not have been considered a candidate for SA, as we call it."

Caroline was shocked. "Are you that selective? Is my awakening a threat to you?"

"Of course not," Cassion said, taking her hand in his as a sign of comfort. "On our planet, as well as on Earth since our arrival, cancer is no longer the dreaded disease it once was. A vaccine has been developed that is given to children at the same time as all the other vaccines. For our scientists, we are interested in the effect your cancer had on your body, how you were able to survive it and still be able to take advantage of the SA offered by the cryogenics lab."

"I'm not certain how to answer you. Can I have some time to speak with my family as well as my employer about this?"

"We would never pressure you," Hodia commented. "We will be in the area on other business until the end of the week. Will that give you enough time to come to a decision?"

"Y-yes, I think so. This is all so new to me."

"Please don't be overly concerned. We will come back here on Friday to get your answer."

With that, Cassion and Hodia left her office.

In a state of shock, Caroline watched as the couple walked down the hall toward the reception desk and disappeared from her view. She fought the urge to lock her office door. Instead, she sank into her chair and engaged her communicator, placing a call to Aaron.

"Caroline?" he answered. "Is something wrong? You're pale as a ghost."

"I just had some visitors at my office. Can you come back here?"

"I was just finishing up here and planning to come back. I can be there in about twenty minutes. Will you be all right until I get there?"

"I-I think I will. I want to go home and..." she allowed the rest of her sentence to trail off. She had no idea what she wanted at this point.

"I'll be there as soon as I can."

The connection closed and she placed a call to Tom at his office.

"What's wrong, Caroline?" he greeted her.

"I don't know if anything is wrong, but I've called Aaron to come back to the library. Can you meet us at my place when you've finished work?"

"Do you want me to come now?"

"No, Tom. I'm certain you have clients you need to see. Tonight will be soon enough. I'd like you to bring Nora as well. What I need to talk about is something that will affect the entire family."

With the connection broken, Caroline got to her feet to close and lock her office door before once again seating herself behind her desk. Had her visitors actually been aliens? They certainly didn't look anything like the pictures of grey aliens she remembered seeing before she made the decision to put her body into suspended animation.

Her memories were of small creatures with gigantic eyes and nondescript features. The people who were just in her office were tall and stately. Their eyes were violet and almost hypnotic. As far as looking any different from the other inhabitants of Earth, they were each dressed in the latest fashions.

What did I expect? she silently questioned. *Did I think they would be wearing nondescript jumpsuits?*

She could hardly believe that twenty minutes passed when she heard a knock at her locked door.

"W-who is it?"

"Caroline, it's me, Aaron."

It was surprising how shaky her legs felt when she got to her feet to unlock the door for Aaron.

"My god, Caroline, what's happened to you? Who were the visitors you mentioned? Did they harm you?"

Unable to put coherent words to her chaotic thoughts, she handed him the two business cards left by Cassion and Hodia.

Once Aaron read the information written on the cards, the color drained from his face. "Are these the people who visited you?"

She nodded, still unable to speak.

"These are two of the most important people in the Council of Intergalactic Affairs. Why did they come here?"

"They-they want me to come to Denver to meet with their doctors for some tests to understand how I was able to survive the suspended animation process. They said I should have never been a candidate for the process in the first place."

"We'll get to the bottom of this. For now, let's get you home so you can call Tom."

"I already called him. For now, I just want to go home and try to figure out what to do about this."

Aaron took care of closing down Caroline's computer as well as turning out the lights and locking the door. At the front desk, he informed the receptionist that Caroline wasn't feeling well and he was taking her home to rest for the remainder of the day.

Their flight took only a matter of minutes and when he dropped her off at her condo, he went to leave his hovercraft at the docking area of his condo. It didn't take long for him to return to her unit.

"Is there anything I can fix you?" he asked.

"Maybe a cup of tea, but I can get it myself."

"Nonsense. I do know how to make tea. As a matter of fact, I'm a relatively good cook. All I need is my communicator and the information for a restaurant that delivers."

She laughed at his statement.

"What's so funny?"

"Even though Adam's parents ran a successful restaurant, that was what he always told me. He used to say he could see no need to learn how to cook, when his parents were so good at it."

She remained seated while Aaron puttered around in her kitchen. When he returned, he carried two mugs of steaming tea.

"What are you going to tell them when they return?" Aaron finally asked.

"I don't know. I have a feeling it's very unusual for the aliens to invite people like me to their medical facility. Back in the twentieth century, there were a lot of stories about alien abductions where people insisted they were taken aboard spaceships and had medical procedures performed on them. Do they want me to be used as a lab rat? Will my life be in danger?"

Before Aaron could answer, the doorbell rang announcing Tom

and Nora's arrival.

While Aaron arranged for dinner to be delivered for the four of them, Caroline filled Tom and Nora in on the visitors who had come to her office earlier in the day.

"Those two people are heavy hitters, if you get my drift," Tom said. "Are you certain you got their names right?"

Caroline reached into her purse and produced the business cards she'd been given earlier in the day. Thankfully, she'd remembered to bring them with her when they left the library. It wasn't until Tom turned the card over that she realized the back side of the card was a hologram that depicted the couple who had been in her office.

"My god, Caroline," Tom began. "These people are as well-known as any of the celebrities or politicians you see on the nightly news. I'm afraid of what might happen when they come back to see you on Friday. I want to be there with you. I think Kirsten should be there as well. As the doctor who first examined you, it's only right."

Before Caroline could comprehend what Tom meant, he was already placing a call to Kirsten on his communicator. She was able to monitor the call and see the expression on her niece's face.

"I wondered when the news of Aunt Caroline's miraculous return to life would be monitored by the Council of Intergalactic Affairs."

"As the first doctor on the scene, you should be with us on Friday when these people come to meet with Caroline."

"Honestly, Tom," Caroline interrupted, "do you really think that is necessary?"

"I agree with Dad," Kirsten said. "Considering why they are coming, I think I should be with you. I can answer many of their questions. I would also want to go with you to Denver. If for no other reason than to look out for your best interests. I doubt there will be any problem catching a shuttle to Chicago tomorrow morning. It's still early enough that I can clear everything with my superiors."

They talked for a few more minutes with Caroline protesting the necessity of Kirsten returning to Chicago. Being outnumbered, she finally agreed that, perhaps, it would be for the best.

~ * ~

For the remainder of the week, Caroline went to work each day, but did not leave her office door unlocked. Her encounter with the aliens on Tuesday left her apprehensive.

Finally, it was Friday. Tom took off work and accompanied her, along with Kirsten, when she went to the library for the day.

It was almost noon when Caroline began to feel like a caged lion. She didn't like the idea of having to wait for the mysterious couple to come back into her life.

"Let's go down to the cafeteria and get some lunch," Aaron suggested when he stopped by the office. "The last time they came here, it was in the afternoon. It's possible they'll be running under the same schedule today."

She knew he made sense, but her stomach was in such knots, eating held no appeal. If the truth be told, she'd hardly eaten anything since her first meeting with the representatives from the Council of Intergalactic Affairs three days earlier.

Once at the cafeteria, she chose a cup of soup and a small packet of crackers.

"You need to eat more than that," Kirsten prompted. "Who knows how long it will be before you are able to get another meal once you go with Cassion and Hodia."

"This will be fine," Caroline assured her niece. "I know my body and at this point trying to eat anything more substantial might end up with me being sick."

While her family and Aaron shook their heads in dismay, they made no further attempt to get her to eat more than what she'd taken earlier.

Her concern over what would happen once she went with the two aliens who were planning to come and get her sometime this afternoon made the French onion soup, which was her favorite, lose its appeal.

After a strained lunch, they returned to Caroline's office. To

Caroline it felt as though she was part of a morbid parade. *Is this how prisoners who were scheduled to death so many years earlier felt as they made their way to the gallows?*

Cassion and Hodia were waiting for them when they reached the office.

"I hope we haven't kept you waiting," Caroline said.

She realized her voice sounded much more relaxed than she was feeling.

"We were certain you had gone down to the cafeteria for the midday meal. It was inconsiderate of us not to tell you exactly when we would be arriving at your office," Hodia said.

Caroline wondered if it was her imagination or if the woman's tone had softened from their first meeting. Still contemplating her assumption, she pulled the key from her pocket and proceeded to unlock the door.

Once they entered the office, she made what she felt were the necessary introductions.

"It is a pleasure to meet all of you. I was hoping you would be here, Mr. Jamison. You too, Dr. Jamison. We are certain you know of our plans to take Caroline with us to our medical facility in Denver. After doing more research, we would appreciate it if the two of you also accompany us."

Although Caroline knew Kirsten was planning to go with her, whether she was invited or not, the indication they wanted Tom to accompany her as well, was shocking.

"Why would you want my daughter, to say nothing of myself, to go with you to Denver?"

"Perhaps it would be for the best if we sat down and made ourselves comfortable," Hodia began. "After much research, we have learned your entire family is descended from what people referred to as 'The Gods.' I'm certain we are correct in assuming all three of you, as well as your brother, Ms. Lewis, are or were left-handed."

Caroline was shocked. "I am, so was my brother. My mother said it was a trait passed down from our father's side of the family. I always thought of it as more of a curse than a blessing."

Hodia laughed at her statement. "On our home planet, being right-handed is the curse. Everything is made to fit the left-handed population. To be right-handed is very rare. Of course, I've gotten off the subject. Many millennia ago, travelers came from planets like ours to help the ancient populations to learn the mysteries of medicine, language and mathematics. They did mate with the indigenous people and left behind descendants all over your planet. Those strains of DNA did not manifest themselves for many generations. To be truthful, it wasn't until the last two hundred years when the left-handed trait became more common worldwide. It was something that remained dormant until the time was right. It was all in preparation for our return to your planet."

"Why return here at all?" Tom asked. "Wasn't your work done here in the ancient past?"

"That is one of the questions that will be answered once you arrive in Denver," Cassion replied. "For now, we need to leave, as our shuttle is waiting for us. I'm certain you will have to make some arrangements before you will be able to accompany us. The same is true for you, Dr. Jamison. While Ms. Lewis will be accompanying Hodia, I will make arrangements for a separate shuttle for myself, Mr. Jamison and Dr. Jamison."

Caroline studied the expression on her nephew's face. Before she could make a comment, it was Kirsten who spoke up.

"I planned on accompanying Aunt Caroline. All of the arrangements have been made with my superiors. I am pleased to think you will welcome my presence."

Both of the aliens nodded their approval.

Chapter Twelve

The transportation system of this new world no longer overwhelmed Caroline. After the bags with the things both she and Kirsten had packed were loaded in the hovercraft parked at the docking station, she kissed Aaron goodbye and took her seat.

Aaron promised he would keep an eye on her condo while she was gone and Tom assured Caroline and Kirsten, he would be joining them as soon as he could pack a bag, make arrangements at the office and let Nora know what was going on.

Although they all shared the same passenger compartment of the craft, the trip to Denver was made in silence. Caroline didn't know if Hodia's silence was because she wasn't allowed to say anything about what would happen at the hospital or if they were all at a loss for words. Unable to stand it much longer, Caroline decided to institute the conversation.

"What prompted the return of your people to Earth at this time?"

Hodia looked at her skeptically at first then nodded. "You have every right to ask this question. For you, I'm certain your memory of history has stopped at the beginning of the pandemic that encompassed the entire world. Unfortunately, in the midst of all of it, there was a lot of political and racial unrest. We watched as things progressed from bad to worse. It was at that time, the One God instructed us intervene. By the time we arrived, the pandemic had run its course but the unrest was still a major problem."

"Unrest?" Kirsten questioned. "I never learned about that in school."

"Of course you didn't. The powers that be in the United States decided that this part of history, like so many others, needed to be erased. We argued long and hard for complete transparency. Unfortunately, we weren't as persuasive as we would have liked. There are times when it's best to choose your battles. Erasing history was the least of our worries when it came to saving this planet."

"What history was erased?" Caroline asked.

"Let's see, slavery, the Holocaust, the Korean War, the Vietnam War, Desert Storm, 9/11, racial unrest, the list goes on and on."

Caroline was horrified. "I remember people saying the Holocaust, as well as when the men first walked on the moon, never happened. I wasn't born at the time of either of these events, but I did know they happened. I was lucky to have enjoyed learning world and U.S. history when I was in high school as well as in college."

"What are the two of you talking about?" Kirsten inquired. "I've never heard of any of those things."

"That's because the powers that be decided no one needed to know about those dark times in history. I have never agreed with this, but like my colleagues, my instructions are to guide and suggest but not to interfere. If you are truly interested in learning the forbidden history, Dr. Jamison, I am certain you will be given access to the facility's library. There are many books there depicting the history of not only the United States, but also the world."

Caroline relaxed against the plush seat, hardly able to comprehend what Hodia was telling them. In her memory, all of the things Hodia mentioned rushed to the forefront. Before she made the decision to be frozen, she recalled the race riots. Many of the incidents had been played and replayed on the nightly news for years before the pandemic hit.

In all of the research she'd done about the coming of the aliens, she'd never found anything about the race riots Hodia described. Had history been intentionally erased? Were the members of this generation as well as several past ones ignorant of what once transpired not only in the United states but around the world?

"How could so much history be forgotten?" she finally asked

Hodia.

"That's what our people have been asking ever since our arrival in the mid twenty-first century. It is one reason why the libraries at our facilities around the world are so important. It isn't just in the United States where history has been altered. It has happened throughout the many countries of Earth. In the Middle East, it started when ISIS destroyed many of the important historical places throughout the area."

"I remember that. At the time, I was horrified. So many irreplaceable artifacts were lost, including many of the writings found in Babylonia. As I recall, I was always fascinated by the history of that area, not only what I read in the Bible, but also the discovery of the Dead Sea Scrolls and many of the other documents that surfaced in Egypt as well as Ethiopia. Those discoveries caused a lot of controversy even though many of them authenticated the writings from the Old Testament."

"I do know about those discoveries," Kirsten added. "Grandpa Jamison told me stories about the documents that were discovered and have been housed in Israel."

Hodia nodded. "Those writings were a great discovery. The One God decided it was the right time for them to be found. My ancestors were living at our complexes both on the dark side of the moon and beneath the ice cap of the seventh continent at the time. From those two places they were able to monitor what was taking place on the surface of Earth. It was their hope their discovery would bring about the peace The One God desired for this planet. Unfortunately, the years that followed produced more political and social unrest. It took many more years of unrest before He deigned the time to be right for us to make our presence known."

Caroline was in shock at what Hodia was telling them. All her life she'd heard theories about alien bases on both the dark side of the moon and under the ice cap of Antarctica. In the last few minutes those theories had been proven correct. The aliens hadn't "come back" to Earth, because it was now evident, they'd never left.

Hodia excused herself to go to the cockpit to talk to the pilot.

"Do you believe what she just told us?" Kirsten asked.

Caroline nodded. "At the beginning of the twenty-first century there was a show on television called 'Ancient Aliens.' Many of the things she told us were speculated upon by the producers of that program. I enjoyed watching it and asking 'what if' whenever those theories were aired. My husband told me I was being foolish, but I didn't agree with him. Now it seems as though I was right, only it's too late for me to tell him and gloat over being right."

"What about the other things she mentioned? I've never heard of the Holocaust and other than World War I and World War II, I had no idea there had been any other conflicts. Another thing I find hard to believe is political, social and racial unrest."

"Oh, my dear, I'm afraid Hodia is right. The history of our nation as well as the world has been rewritten. In my day there was a saying that we should learn from the mistakes of the past. When things are erased history is doomed to repeat itself. The Holocaust took place during World War II. A man by the name of Adolf Hitler became the ruler of Germany and deemed it necessary to destroy all of the people of Jewish descent as well as the Gypsies that lived in Eastern Europe. They were taken to concentration camps. Once there, many of them were executed and dumped into mass graves. Others were taken into what they thought were shower rooms and were gassed before they were burned in the ovens. It was a dark time in history, but many people wanted to believe it never happened."

"How horrible. Why could people not believe it happened?"

"I've always wondered about the same thing. It was something too horrifying to contemplate. Many people said that things like that couldn't happen in the United States, but during World War II there were citizens of Japanese descent who were rounded up and taken to internment camps. They weren't exterminated, but they were treated as though they were responsible for the Japanese attack on Pearl Harbor, Hawaii."

Before she could continue with the history lesson, Hodia returned to tell them they should prepare for docking in Denver.

~ * ~

The facility in Denver far surpassed anything Caroline could have imagined. The hospital in Chicago where she was taken when she first awakened was, in her opinion, state of the art, but it looked primitive in comparison.

"Welcome, Ms. Lewis," a tall stately-looking woman in a white lab coat greeted her. "I'm Dr. Aragon. I have been monitoring your arrival in the twenty-second century ever since the news of your discovery was made public. To be truthful, your family has been followed by our people as well as the One God for two centuries."

"I'd appreciate it if you called me Caroline. It's far less formal. May I ask you a question?"

"We are prepared to be completely transparent. What is it that you want to know?"

Caroline swallowed hard, contemplating the question that had been nagging at her mind ever since Hodia first mentioned the fact that left-handed people were "of the Gods." "From what I know of my ancestry, I wonder how I could be called 'of the Gods'?"

"That is a perfectly logical question. Before every child is born, the spirit of that child is held in the hands of The One God. Along with the DNA from their parents, some children are blessed with the gift of being left-handed. Throughout the generations this has been looked upon as a curse, but it was a link to those of us who have been monitoring Earth for many millennia. Usually, there is only one child in a family with this blessing, but in the case of your family, the One God deemed it necessary to bestow the gift on more than one left-handed person. Everything in your life has been monitored and followed closely. Even your decision to be frozen at the cryogenics lab was approved of by The One God. When the others were lost when the disasters hit the west coast, you were spared to be resurrected at this time in history. Your memories of the past are something the people of this century need to hear and learn from."

The information Dr. Aragon imparted shook Caroline to the core. "I know my brother was left-handed, as are Tom and Kirsten, but what do they have to do with this master plan of yours?"

"Before the disaster that took place on the east and west coasts, your brother was warned in a dream to leave California and return to the Midwest in order to save his family."

"Warned in a dream? That sounds a bit like the story of Joseph being warned to take Mary and Jesus to Egypt to escape the wrath of King Herod."

Dr. Aragon laughed. "It seems you know your Biblical history quite well. The story of Jesus as well as much of the Old Testament is totally true. Of course, the historians who wrote those stories didn't take into account the actual age of the Earth."

"I've often wondered about the whole God thing. I realize the God of the Hebrews, the Muslims and the Christians originated through Abraham but what about the other religions of the world?"

"The One God can take many different forms. He is the ruler of the Universe, not just Earth and the planets of this solar system. Never underestimate the power he holds in his hands."

She hadn't realized how late it was but Dr. Aragon held out her hand.

"You must be tired from your trip here. I have been informed that your nephew and Cassion have arrived and are waiting for us to join them for the evening meal. Once you are finished, you will be taken to your quarters. Tomorrow we will be starting your testing. Therefore, you will need your rest."

~ * ~

Kirsten, Tom, Hodia and Cassion waited for her in what looked like a medieval dining room in an ancient castle, stranger than anything Caroline was familiar with. The table was set with fine china, crystal and silverware with candelabra at either end of the table as well as in the center. Although they didn't hold the traditional candles, they gave off a warm glow that filled the room with an ambiance of a long-forgotten age.

"I was worried about where you went," Kirsten greeted her. "Even though Hodia assured me you were in good hands, I was concerned."

"There was no need. Dr. Aragon was most gracious and we talked about the history of our planet. I hope you were also well taken care of."

"I was. Once Dad and Cassion arrived, we were given a tour of this facility. As a physician, I would give anything to work in a hospital as well equipped as this one."

"Kirsten is right," Tom said. "I was equally impressed by the law library. I'm anxious to meet with some of the lawyers and learn everything I can from them. I realize there will be some medical testing, but I've been assured there will be time for me to meet with their attorneys."

Caroline wished she was as comfortable with the circumstances of her being brought to Denver as were Tom and Kirsten. She worried about what the next few days would bring. Would she become a lab rat or be treated like an honored guest?

Chapter Thirteen

Caroline awoke in a strange room. It took a moment for her to get her bearings and realize this room was the one the aliens brought her to last night after they finished dinner. She'd expected to be taken to a hospital room like the one she occupied in Chicago after her return from the dead. Instead, the room was more like a palatial suite in a high-class hotel.

She'd been given a gown, but it wasn't the usual hospital gown with the opening in the back. This one was of luxurious silk in a flattering shade of lavender. It was amazing to think there were clothes in the room's closet that were the perfect size. How did they know what to have there for her?

While she brought herself to full awareness, she remembered a dream she'd experienced prior to awaking. She'd forgotten about the medications she took prior to going to the cryogenics lab. As she recalled, she was taking medication for her missing thyroid and was told she would be taking it for the rest of her life.

Technically, her life stopped when she entered into the contract to have her body frozen to be revived in the future. Had something happened during her prolonged sleep that negated the reason to take the medication?

A knock at the door ceased her mental ramblings. She quickly picked up the matching robe to her gown. It was conveniently draped over the chair just a few inches away from the head of the bed.

When she opened the door, she was greeted by Dr. Aragon, Hodia and Kirsten. "I hope we didn't waken you," Dr. Aragon greeted her.

The statement brought a smile to Caroline's lips. With the

technology of the twenty-second century, she was certain they knew every move she'd made since entering the room the evening before.

"No, I've been awake for a few minutes. It always takes me a while before I'm ready to get dressed for the day."

"We thought it would be fun to join you in your suite for breakfast, Aunt Caroline," Kirsten said. "We'll go into the sitting room while you get dressed. We ordered the food and it should be delivered in about a half an hour."

Caroline nodded her agreement and went to the bathroom for her morning shower. By the time she finished and was dressed for the day, she heard the three women in the sitting room talking among themselves.

At the dining table, four places had been set. She no more than took her seat when the food was delivered. The array of dishes made her feel as though she was at one of the Sunday buffet brunches she and Adam frequented throughout their marriage.

"This looks like a feast fit for a queen," she observed. "It's amazing that you were able to arrange for all of my favorites."

"Most of the choices were ones Kirsten made," Hodia replied. "It seems as though we all enjoy the same things when it comes to choices for breakfast."

After filling her plate with fluffy pancakes, bacon, and fresh fruit, Caroline took her first taste of the food. In the back of her mind she decided the only thing missing was the champagne. Before she could comment, Hodia handed her a glass of fresh squeezed orange juice. After the first taste, she realized it was a mimosa. It soon became evident the champagne mixed with the juice was of the best quality.

"I'm surprised," she exclaimed. "I certainly didn't expect anything like this here."

"Do you mean the champagne?" Hodia asked.

Caroline nodded.

"Let me answer your question," Dr. Aragon replied. "This is a research facility, not a hospital. Through our belief in the One God, we realize wine or other spirits are not sinful nor something to be looked down upon. These are gifts from our maker and if used in moderation, there is no problem. It is the same with food or anything else. None of these things become a problem unless they are abused. Since our arrival on your planet, we have learned the lessons of the One God who sent his son here. He did the same thing on our planet at an earlier time in our history. Over the millennia the people have strayed, but finally come back to the belief that rules our lives, no matter where we have traveled."

Caroline took another sip of her drink and tasted the tempting food on her plate. "That brings up another question. In the twentieth century, I learned how many light-years the planets in our solar systems are away from each other. I've also heard about suspended animation. Is this anything like cryogenics?"

Hodia laughed at the question Caroline posed. "I wondered how long it would take for you to ask this question. The answer is yes, it is a crude form of what our people have perfected. When the One God realized you were of the gods and decided to take this drastic step to save your life, He stepped in to make certain your body was perfectly preserved for a future generation to discover. It is the reason you survived the natural disasters that struck the west coast of this country."

"Before you ask your next question, let me expand on what Hodia said," Dr. Aragon interjected. "Based on the information found at the cryogenics lab, we know you have had cancer, not once but twice. One of the things I'm certain you have found perplexing is the lack of the medication you once took. We know you were taking a pill because of your breast cancer and were to do so for five years after your recovery. You no longer take it because more than five years have passed. Next is the medication I am certain you thought you would be taking for your thyroid for the rest of your natural life. First, you have exceeded your natural life and second, the technology, no matter how primitive it may seem to us, accidentally developed a situation where your body has compensated for your lack of a thyroid. This said, your body has healed itself. If I am not mistaken, we will find the thyroid has regenerated. It's not something that happens naturally, but only through the grace of the One God. In all of history of this or any other planet that serves the One God, you are the only one who has had such a healing take place."

Caroline was in awe. She was no one special. She's taken the coward's way out and opted to have her body frozen rather than take a chance of contracting the virus that took her husband's life.

"You've given me a lot to think about. Not only my physical condition, but also what has happened to the history of our world. I realize my life was spared for some reason, even though I don't know what it was. Is there something I can do to rectify what has been lost over the generations?"

Around the table her companions continued to eat in silence as though contemplating what she was proposing.

"There was a reason you were brought here and I'm certain you have the correct concept of it. You have been watched by our people ever since you were awakened. Your knowledge of what we perceive as 'ancient history' is invaluable. Combined with our knowledge of what has transpired since our return to Earth and the reason for it, this will prove highly beneficial to all of the future generations."

Caroline was speechless. She was no one special. Why had all of this happened to her? When she decided on going to the cryogenics lab, it was out of desperation. With Adam gone and no children to give her comfort, she thought it was the best thing to do. The pandemic was just beginning and she was afraid she would catch it and die a horrible death. Never in her wildest dreams did she expect to awaken in a world where no one knew the history, not only of the United States, but also of the world.

"What do you think I can do?" she finally managed to ask.

"Whether you know it or not, you are a celebrity," Hodia replied. "We have been monitoring many places including the government, and some say you are a national treasure, while there are those who feel you are a threat because of the information of the past you possess. One of the reasons you are here is for us to glean whatever information you can provide as well as to give you the security you need until we can contact the proper people in the government who will best be able to handle this information and protect you."

"I've never considered myself anyone other than my husband's wife and business partner. It's going to take me a long time for me to come to grips with this new identity."

~ * ~

With the breakfast meeting completed, Caroline followed Dr. Aragon to an office that looked more like a recording studio than a doctor's office.

"For the duration of your stay with us, this will be your personal office. Each morning you will be given an event from history. We would like you to record everything you know on that topic. Once you are finished, you will be free to explore the complex, but not to leave the grounds."

"Are you certain I'm in danger?"

"Not certain, but from the information we've gathered, there are people who would rather you didn't confirm the history the government doesn't want released."

"What about the tests I was told would be run?"

"The DNA chip that was placed in your body when you were first discovered has been scanned and provided a wealth of information. Before I leave I will take a blood sample for the remainder of our tests."

"I don't remember a chip being placed in my body."

"Of course, you wouldn't. I spoke with Kirsten yesterday and she said it was a normal procedure and was done while you were still dazed by the effects of the suspended animation."

"I guess that makes sense."

"I'm sure it doesn't, but for now we have left you your first assignment."

Caroline picked up the notebook that was laying on the desk. The label on the outside cover read "VIETNAM WAR." Although she hadn't been born when it was going on, she remembered her father telling her stories of when he was in the Marines and served three tours of duty in that pointless war.

After Dr. Aragon taught her how to use the recording equipment, she left Caroline alone in the room, with her thoughts about where to begin to verify the history that had been lost.

Finally, she started.

"My father served three tours of duty in Vietnam. They were supposed to be there to stop the communist North Vietnamese from taking over the entire country. It was a war that should have never happened, or at least, one the United States shouldn't have been involved in."

It was well past noon when she shut off the recorder. She was amazed by how much information she'd retained from her father's stories and the classes she'd taken in high school and college. She prayed she would be able to pull similar information from the recesses of her brain regarding the other historical events these people were interested in learning about.

~ * ~

Knowing she'd missed lunch, Caroline went back to her suite and changed to more formal clothes for dinner with her family.

She'd just finished dressing when Cassion knocked on her door.

"Are you ready for dinner?" he greeted her.

"I most certainly am. I was so engrossed in what I was doing, I forgot all about lunch."

A scowl crossed his face. "That is not good. In the future, I will make certain lunch will be delivered to you while you are working. I have listened to the recording you made and have to say I'm thrilled about what you have recorded regarding the Vietnam War. If your other memories are as clear as these, we will have enough information to contact the government with our request to reinstate the lost history of, not only the United States, but also the world."

"When did all of this begin?"

Cassion stopped mid-stride and turned toward her. "From what we can ascertain, it was in the early twenty-first century that some of the history of this country was deleted from many of the high school history classes. During the pandemic and the racial unrest that came at the same time, many of the statues depicting the history of this country were torn down. It was as if people thought history could be changed by tearing down the monuments that were reminders of times people didn't want to remember. That is why your memories are so important."

"I see. As I recall, I was always enamored with history. Although I never used it, I did major in history in college. After I met my husband, I realized I would become his partner in business, where I wouldn't have a need for my background in history. I never thought I might be one of the only people who remembered things that everyone else wanted to forget."

Their conversation came to an end when they reached the dining room. Tom and Kirsten waited for her and she knew they would be anxious to tell of their adventures of their first full day at the complex.

"How was your day?" Tom inquired.

"It was tiring. How was yours?"

"Interesting, to say the very least. I learned some interesting things about my great-grandfather. The reason he left California and returned to Chicago was information planted in his subconscious by the aliens. They knew about the disasters that were about to hit the west coast and wanted to make certain the family continued throughout the generations. I also learned that you were spared by the aliens for the same reason. It seems like they believe in the same God as we do and He had plans for our entire family. I was given several passages from the Bible to read. I must say they were very enlightening."

Cassion and Hodia joined them in the dining room, making their private conversation impossible.

Like the evening before, the meal they were served was a lavish affair. Each course was more delicious than the one that preceded it. Most of the dishes were ones she recognized but some were so exotic Caroline wondered what it was she'd eaten.

Chapter Fourteen

The next few days seemed to be a carbon copy of the first full day Caroline spent at the complex.

Each morning Hodia and Kirsten would join her for breakfast, before Caroline returned to the office assigned to her to record the history she remembered about many of the events of, not only the twentieth and twenty-first centuries, but the many things in the history she'd studied in college.

It always amazed her how much of the history she'd studied so many years earlier came back to her as soon as she read the first identifying words. Facts she thought were long forgotten or hidden in the dark recesses of her mind came to the forefront, reminding her how much she always loved history.

She'd been at the complex for almost two weeks, when Hodia and Cassion came to her office. She was caught completely off guard when they said they had something serious to discuss with her.

"What could be so serious? Has something happened to Tom or Kirsten?"

"No, they are safe, but your friend Aaron has been taken into custody by the military faction that is in direct conflict with the government."

"Aaron? Why?"

Cassion had a worried expression on his face. "From what our agents can ascertain, they were looking for information about your whereabouts. He's been taken to a secure location, although we aren't certain where it is. Our agents are working on getting him released to their custody. They have also learned that your condo was broken into and ransacked. It is entirely possible they were looking for information regarding where you went. We know the current administration isn't involved. The information we've uncovered is that the militants are hoping by finding you they can suppress the truth of the past and continue without teaching the history they don't want the people to know."

Caroline was horrified by the information Cassion just imparted to her. "I thought things were bad when I decided to submit to the cryogenics. If this government is less corrupt, how can any of this be happening?"

"We thought so too, but it seems there is a militant organization influencing those who are in power. They are not necessarily trying to influence the president, but we fear they have invaded the department of education. We have long realized the suppression of the information regarding this world's history has been perpetuated since the late twentieth century, but we never had a way to substantiate everything until you virtually came back from the dead. I'm afraid you are in danger unless you remain here."

"What about Aaron?"

"I can answer that," Hodia replied. "Our agents are working on finding where he is being held. Once he is located, he will be brought here for his safety until those responsible for this can be captured and brought to justice."

"Are we prisoners here?"

"Hardly." Cassion sounded shocked at her accusation. "You, as well as Tom's family and Aaron, will be here to be protected from the fraction that wants you along with the history of the past to be eliminated. It shouldn't take long for the wrongs to be made right and those responsible prosecuted."

Caroline wanted to take comfort in Cassion's promise, but concern for Aaron's safety was uppermost in her mind.

~ * ~

By evening, Nora and Kevin had joined them in protective custody. Only Aaron was missing. It seemed as though the agents Cassion spoke of earlier had not been successful in finding where he was being held.

"This is all my fault," Caroline lamented as soon as they were seated in the dining room for the evening meal. "If I hadn't been brought back to life, none of this would have happened. I am so sorry to have put you all in danger."

"Don't talk like that," Nora said consolingly. "I was called by the condo association after the break-in. They wanted me to assess the damage and see what, if anything, had been taken. Other than the things I helped you pack for the trip here, nothing was missing, but the couch cushions were slashed and your belongings were strewn all over the place. When one of Cassion's agents contacted me, I was more than ready to come with him."

"It was the same with me, Aunt Caroline," the young man who sat next to Kirsten said. "When I told my boss what was going on, he told me to go to where I was safe. My job will be waiting for me when this mess is cleared up. I'm more worried about Aaron than my position with the company I work for in Texas."

Kevin's comment put Caroline at ease, albeit with the concern of not knowing where Aaron was being held.

They continued their conversation before Hodia joined them. "We have news," she announced. "We have found where they are holding Aaron. From what we have learned, he is being treated well. By going through proper channels, it is possible his captors will be arrested and he will be brought here no later than tomorrow evening."

"If that's so, will this be over?" Kevin asked.

"Unfortunately, no. This group is only a minute portion of a much larger cell of terrorists who are intent on corrupting the government of this country. Hopefully, those we take into custody will be able to lead us to the others who are organizing this faction."

Cassio's use of the words cell of terrorists, brought back memories of the 9/11 attacks on New York, Washington, D.C. and the plane that crashed in Pennsylvania. Caroline felt her hopes being dashed. She was beginning to doubt whether or not she would be returning to her condo and the life she'd been building for herself in the Chicago area.

~ * ~

The next morning, Caroline picked up her assignment, but her heart wasn't into the work. In her mind, she dwelled on Aaron and what was happening with him. What if he wasn't found? Would the militants torture him to learn of her whereabouts? Was she that much of a threat that the militants wanted the past, the history of this country as well as the world erased or even changed?

"Are you all right?" Hodia asked before she left Caroline's office.

"I don't think so. What will the people who are holding Aaron do to him? Is his life in danger because of me? Are my memories that frightening to them?"

Hodia thought for a moment before replying. "I doubt that Aaron is in danger. It's entirely possible our people are already negotiating for his release. As for what frightens the militants, you have to go back into ancient history to understand what their motives are. Rather than work on your assignment, I suggest you come with me to the library. There is an essay there that was written by one of my ancestors, shortly after they made their presence known to the people of this planet. Unfortunately, they were too late to repair much of the damage that was done during the riots that erupted at the height of the pandemic of 2020. This is why your return to the future has been such a boon to the entire world. With what has been destroyed, your memories can restore much of what has been lost."

Caroline could hardly believe what she was hearing.

"I've been back from my induced sleep for several months now. I've even been working as a resource librarian. How could all of this have escaped me?"

"I can understand your concerns. There is an old saying, 'you don't miss what you don't have.' Why would you question the lack of history when the people who questioned you were only interested in things like fashion and socially acceptable behavior in the twentieth and twenty-first centuries? I do believe you will glean a better understanding by reading THE ERASURE OF THE PAST."

Caroline nodded and left her assignment for the day lying on her desk. The thought of reading what happened in the past drew her like a magnet.

~ * ~

THE ERASURE OF THE PAST

My name does not matter, I only hope to shed light on what was happening on this planet called Earth, beginning in the late twentieth century and continuing for many years.

It all started, at least I think it all started, after the Vietnam War. The Americans were not all in favor of their country's involvement in that war. It is evident they equated it with the Korean Conflict of the 1950s. Both were wars within a country far from their borders. Many young men and women lost their lives and the people were angry. They wanted to move on and worry only about what was happening within their borders.

By the latter part of the twentieth century, both of these conflicts where glossed over. Students were not taught about them or why their country involved itself in something that was not a threat to them.

In 2001, 9/11 hit home and hit home hard. The Americans saw that war had come to their country. They were no longer fighting communism. A new threat was at their doorstep. They decided it was the Taliban in Afghanistan and the government of one of the Middle Eastern countries who were behind the attacks on the World Trade Center in New York, as well as the Pentagon in Washington, D.C. and the crash of a commercial aircraft into a field in Pennsylvania.

Once again, the United States was involved in wars far from their homes that were taking their young men and women into combat situations.

On the home front, elected officials suddenly became more

interested in their political parties and their views, rather than what was right and good for the people they represented. Political campaigns didn't lay out the party platform or the ideals of people running for office. Instead, they spread lies and misinformation about their opponents. They promised things that couldn't be obtained and led the people to believe in projects that were unnecessary and too draining on the economy.

In 2020 the world was looking forward to a new decade, a new beginning. Instead there was a threat of nuclear war. Within two months the concern wasn't about missiles but an invisible threat called COVID-19 invaded the entire world.

Many thought it was germ warfare, others called it a plague sent from the One God. Whatever it was, it changed the world entirely. Some countries reacted to it immediately and put protective measures in place. Others didn't take the threat seriously, resulting in the huge loss of life, before a vaccine could be produced to become the savior for the entire population of the world.

It was during the pandemic that racial tensions threatened to boil over. Although it had been going on for years, the death of a black man in Minnesota ignited a bomb that brought riots to the streets, including killings and lootings.

Statues of many of the men who fought for the South during the Civil War were torn down and names of many places that bore their names were renamed. Statues of other people from history, including Christopher Columbus and Abraham Lincoln, were torn down or defaced. It was a dark time in the history of America.

The main outcome of all the violence and unrest was that history was either erased or rewritten. My prayer is that sometime in the future there will be a savior from the past who will remind, not only the United States, but also the world, of the important happenings of the past.

~ * ~

"Caroline."

The sound of Aaron's voice pulled her attention away from the pages that opened her eyes to so many things that occurred in her country both before and after her decision to enter into a state of suspended animation.

"They were able to rescue you," she said, getting to her feet and hurrying to embrace him.

"I don't know if I'd call it a rescue. I never considered myself to be in any danger, but there was an intense interrogation as to where you'd been taken. It was an uncomfortable situation, but I doubt if it was dangerous. They were more intrusive than abusive. It was a relief when Cassion's men came and insisted I should be released into their custody."

"What were you able to tell them?"

"Nothing, other than Cassion and Hodia came and took you to one of their facilities. Even though I knew where you were taken, I wasn't about to give them the satisfaction of gaining that information from me. Can you tell me what's this all about?"

Caroline weighed her options about revealing any information and yet, since Aaron was here, he needed to know the answer.

"It seems the history I remembered from the past, both from my personal knowledge and what I learned as a history major in college, has been erased. I was horrified to learn most people today know nothing of the past, be it concerning the United States or the other countries of the world."

"What are you talking about?"

"What do you know about the two world wars, the Korean conflict or the war in Vietnam?"

Aaron's expression told her more than she ever wanted to know.

"Other than those things are ancient history, absolutely nothing. History was never my strong suit."

"Well, it's mine. I remember when ISIS destroyed many of the ancient historical sites and artifacts in Iran. The loss of those artifacts was devastating. To think the people of the world have no idea of what went on in the past makes me very sad. From what I read, things like the slavery of the seventeenth, eighteenth and nineteenth centuries has been taken out of the history books, along with the atrocities surrounding the Klu Klux

Klan."

Aaron's look of bewilderment deepened. It was evident he knew absolutely nothing about what history had been erased or changed.

Rather than continuing her work for the day, Caroline decided to spend time with Aaron and her family. With so many unanswered questions, it was best if she tried to get some answers.

~ * ~

"What do you make of all of this?" Kevin asked, once Caroline told the family about the work she'd been doing ever since her arrival in Denver. "Why would anyone want to erase history?"

Caroline smiled at his questions. "In my day, there was a saying, 'if we don't know history, we are destined to repeat it.' I'm certain I'm misquoting but I think you get the idea. I remember when things like this started happening. I was certain it was the only in the Middle East where the destruction was being carried out. Instead, some of the departments of our own government is perpetuating this terrible practice. It's a sin against humanity. How can we better ourselves unless we understand the past?"

"You have a point, Aunt Caroline," Kevin said. "What I want to know is how you can be of assistance?"

"I think you underestimate your aunt," Cassion said, as he entered the room and joined the conversation. "When she made the decision to submit to being put into suspended animation, she possessed the knowledge of not only what happened in the twentieth and early twenty-first centuries, but also of many events of the past. Our forebearers kept track of all of those who were 'of the Gods' and knew of her background, including her history major in college. That said, she is very important to the future generations of this planet. It is imperative they know the truth behind the fabricated history."

"Fabricated?" Caroline questioned. "Don't you mean erased or eradicated?"

Cassion nodded. It was the affirmation she needed.

"Beginning tomorrow, I will be more diligent about my work. For today, I plan to take some time to get to know my grandnephew, several times removed, enjoy Aaron's company and spend the day with my family."

Chapter Fifteen

The next morning, Caroline made a request for information to be brought to her office. Within the hour, she had a stack of history books outlining the curriculum being taught in high schools and colleges around the world.

She spent the better part of the day reading the text and making notes about the discrepancies she found.

"How could they do this?" she asked of no one in particular. "According to this drivel, there were never any race wars and the war between the states was nothing more than a minor disagreement that was settled almost overnight. What a farce."

"Are you upset?" Hodia asked.

The fact that the aliens seemed to be able to appear almost out of nowhere amazed her as much as it always had.

"You bet I'm upset. The Civil War was one of the darkest times in the history of the United States. How can it be classified as a minor disagreement? Many brave men lost their lives on both sides and it wasn't settled overnight as these books suggest. The war and the aftermath, including the actions of organizations like the Klu Klux Klan, ruined the relations between the black and white citizens of this country for almost two hundred years. I can only account for the time before I went to sleep, but I'm certain things didn't end just because I didn't experience them."

"You're right, of course. They didn't. It took the murder of a black man named George Floyd, in Minneapolis, to bring everything to the boiling point. What happened was as wrong as what the politicians did by eradicating the facts of history after the conflict between the races was finally settled and all of the citizens were finally seen as equal."

"How long did it take?"

"It took decades but the eradication of history spanned more years than any of us care to talk about."

"Why didn't you stop them? From what I've read, your historians know the truth."

"We couldn't stop them, since we are the outsiders. Our mission here is to be advisors, but not to interfere. It is a hard job. You are the hope for the future. Since you are a native of this planet, your word cannot be disputed. Once you have finished the work you've been doing, we will arrange a meeting between you and the leaders of the various countries all around the planet."

Caroline hung her head in contemplation of what her role would be in the future of her home planet. "I never considered myself to be an important person. I was my husband's wife and business partner. I never did anything for myself until after I lost the most important reason for my life. It was only then that I made the decision to go to sleep and not be awakened until the pandemic ended. I never thought my return to this would be important to anyone but me."

"You are a humble woman. It's a shame there aren't more people like you in the world. Believe me when I say you are going to be a very important part of the future of this planet. Take your time doing this research. We have more than enough time to finish what you have to do and get in contact with the leaders of the world."

"What about my family and Aaron?"

"They are being debriefed and will soon return to their former lives."

"What do you mean debriefed?"

"They will be given the opportunity to stay here and help you with your work. I know that is what Aaron wants to do. As for your nieces and nephews, they haven't made any decision yet. We are ready to offer each of them positions within our facility in their chosen professions."

Caroline understood what Hodia was saying. By being associated with her, Aaron and her family were all in danger. It was evident to her that Kirsten would be delighted to practice medicine in this ultra-modern facility. As for Kevin, Tom and Nora, the decision would be a much more difficult one to make.

~ * ~

As it had been ever since her arrival, the evening meal was an elegant affair. By the time she arrived, the others were already there.

"This is all so exciting," Kevin said when they finally sat around the table. "I was able to meet with their engineers today and they offered me a position. I can't believe what they offered me in the way of compensation. Other than my apartment in Texas and a few friends, I have nothing to leave behind. Once I accepted their offer, things moved very quickly. My employers were contacted and they wished me well. I was informed my apartment would be packed up and cleaned. I've even been given a new apartment within the complex. As far as my furniture goes, I asked if they could donate it to charity. All I wanted were my personal possessions. My new place has all of the furnishings and they were much better than the ones I purchased at Goodwill and rummage sales."

"I'm also going to be staying here," Kirsten said. "Since my accommodations are little more than a room at the hospital, I was thrilled with the offer to work here. I've been impressed with the facility ever since we arrived. I'm moving into an apartment in the same complex as Kevin."

Caroline smiled. She too had been assigned a condo on the grounds, as had Aaron. It was as though none of their former lives mattered now that they were to become part of this new society.

"That leaves Nora and me," Tom said. "I've also been offered a position. Unlike the rest of you, I won't be doing my work here. Instead, I will continue to work at the firm in Chicago. There is a lot of work that requires someone away from the complex to do on their behalf."

"I've also had news. Since Tom will need extra help at his office, we've made arrangements to sell my condo to one of the attorneys who will be joining him," Aaron commented.

"What about my condo?" Caroline finally asked.

"The offer applies to your condo as well. Of course, your furnishings were destroyed when the militant agents raided your unit."

She could feel her head begin to swim with everything that was happening. How could militant agents break into her condo and ruin all of the furnishings she'd so carefully chosen to depict her personality?

Once again, she damned the pandemic that, in her mind, forced her to make the decision to have her body frozen. If she hadn't taken such drastic measures, she wouldn't have been awakened in 2120. She would have died from either natural or unnatural causes. Had that been the case she would not have endangered her family or Aaron.

What have I done? Will I be able to right the wrongs of the erasure of history? Should I even try?

The answer to her unspoken questions was an enthusiastic yes. History was important, even though those who wanted to forget it didn't think so. She blessed her education and all of the history classes she'd taken and loved. Hopefully she could bring about changes that would be beneficial to those who lived in the twenty-second century and the generations yet to be born.

"Have you had enough time with your family, Caroline?" Dr. Aragon asked, as she entered the room.

"I have, but I feel I am responsible for the changes that are about to take place in their lives, be they for good or bad."

"I assure you, their decisions were not made lightly," Cassion commented, adding his voice to their conversation. "It was Kirsten who approached us about joining the staff of our medical facility. Her resume is impressive and the head of our hospital was thrilled with her request for a transfer. We feel her expertise is being wasted working at a field hospital. She will be a great addition to our staff."

"Cassion is right," Kirsten agreed. "I've wanted to transfer from the field hospital ever since I received the call about the discovery of your perfectly preserved body. This opportunity couldn't have come at a better time. I've been preparing my resume for a transfer, I just didn't know where I would be applying."

Caroline felt a little better knowing the idea of transfer came from Kirsten and had not been insisted on by the aliens.

"It's the same with me, Aunt Caroline," Kevin assured her. "Once I saw their engineering department, I was so impressed, I asked if it would be possible for me to be included. They said they had to check my references, and when they did, I was offered the position. I feel I can make great strides in my chosen field by working here. I've also met many of the people I'll be working with. I thought they would all be aliens, but I soon learned they are some of the top people in the industry. Even the head of the department is a respected engineer from the Albuquerque area. I've read about his accomplishments throughout college and now I will be able to work with him."

She nodded. Both of the younger members of her family seemed enthralled with the idea of working within this complex.

"How will this affect your firm, Tom?"

Her nephew smiled. "It will be a great boon, both through the aspect of the diversity of our clientele but also those of the financial rewards. I've met with the two attorneys who will be joining our firm and they are both Earthlings who have been trained by the aliens to handle the legal dealings for, not only this complex, but others around the country and the world. This is an opportunity I never thought I would be able to attain."

"You've brought great opportunities for our entire family," Nora gushed. "Who would have known that the mythical Aunt Caroline would return from the dead and change all of our lives for the better. Your arrival has opened more new doors than any of us could have ever expected."

Caroline said nothing. She never thought of herself as being either mythical or able to change the lives of those most dear to her. Before subjecting herself to the state of suspended animation, she had considered what her return to the world would be like.

In her mind, she would be reconnected with her brother and his family. Even though she knew she wouldn't age, she would have to cultivate a new group of friends and acquaintances. If her brother had followed her wishes, she would have a good nest egg stored away securely in the bank.

With the exception of being able to see her brother again, the anticipated events came to pass. Unfortunately, she'd been awakened fifty years later than she thought.

"I wonder what my part in this new world will be," she mused.

"I can answer that," Cassion said, joining the conversation. "You are truly not only a national treasure but a gift to the entire planet. Your knowledge of the past, which has been written and rewritten over the past one hundred years, is invaluable. Beginning next week, you will be meeting with many of the world's leaders. The first will be the president of the United States, Brian Addison. When we sent out emails of contact with the leaders, he was the first to reply."

"Should I be concerned about such a meeting? In light of what transpired at my condo and the abduction of Aaron, is President Addison someone to be feared?"

"Not at all," Cassion assured her. "The faction who abducted Aaron was one that is against the current government. For years, President Addison has been saying there is something wrong with the way history is being treated, not only by the United States as well as around the world. I have met with him on various occasions. His election was a shock to those who want to forget what happened in the past. He is behind the archaeological group who found you and has been interested in the knowledge you could impart ever since your discovery was made public. Although it was our superiors who insisted you should be brought here, it was President Addison who also asked us to look into you helping us."

"I feel a bit overwhelmed."

"Please don't be," Hodia assured her. "Just be yourself and you will win over everyone you meet. Everyone here has become very enamored with you in the brief time you have been with us. Now, I do believe our dinner is ready to be served. It would be a snub to the chef if we were to allow the dishes he has worked so hard on to go cold."

Chapter Sixteen

Caroline awoke to the voice of her alarm alerting her to the fact it was seven o'clock on Monday morning and she needed to ready herself for her eleven o'clock appointment with President Addison.

Over the weekend, she had moved from her secure suite at the hospital to what she could only call a palatial condo within the complex. Even with the wealth she'd accumulated over the past one hundred years, she would have never considered purchasing such an ultra-modern place to live.

The furnishings were of the latest design and could have easily cost a small fortune. Everything from the alarm clock to the doors were voice activated. It reminded her of the units that were becoming popular in the early twenty-first century. Back then they were called Siri or Alexa. There had been many rumors of such units eavesdropping on personal conversations and invading people's homes.

When she first encountered all of this modern technology, she questioned the reliability of the electronic invaders. Hodia assured her the glitches to such devices had been eliminated many years earlier and they were no more than a robotic voice meant to help the people of this time with information and assistance.

"If they have information, why do you need me? Surely these robots can answer all of your questions."

Hodia laughed at her inquiry. "The robot is only as good as those who program them. If history has been lost or, as we think, tampered with, these units would not know the truth."

At the time, it all made sense. Now, she wasn't so sure.

Sherry Derr-Wille

After taking her morning shower, she spent extra time to style her hair and put on her makeup. If she was to meet someone as important as the President of the United States, she certainly wanted to look her best.

Assured of her appearance, she went into the kitchen of her condo and made herself toast and coffee to go along with the fresh fruit she found in the refrigeration unit. It wasn't the elaborate breakfast she'd enjoyed while in the hospital, but it was enough to satisfy her. The importance of this morning's meeting had her stomach in knots and her nerves on edge.

~ * ~

Just prior to eleven, a young man announced himself from outside her front door.

"Ms. Lewis, I'm an aide to President Addison and have come to escort you to the meeting that is scheduled between the two of you. My name is Lt. James Corcoran."

Caroline gave the command for the door to open and was impressed by the impeccable appearance of the military man who greeted her. Although his voice sounded much younger, he looked to be in his late thirties. Without prompting, he produced identification, verifying his name and rank.

Comfortable with his identity, she allowed him to take her arm and escort her to the conference room where she would be meeting with the president.

As soon as she entered the room, a man dressed in a suit and tie got to his feet. She took a moment to assess him. He looked to be about her same age, less the one hundred years she'd been asleep. It was hard thinking she was still a forty-two-year-old woman, even though the calendar said differently. She immediately mentally corrected herself. Since her awakening, she'd had a birthday and was now forty-three.

"It's a pleasure to finally meet you," President Addison said, holding out his hand.

"I have a feeling that is what I should be saying to you. Back in my day, a hundred years ago, I would have never envisioned myself meeting someone as important as the President of the United States."

"I wouldn't call myself important. If I've done my research correctly, in 2020, President Donald Trump held my office."

The mention of President Trump made her a bit uneasy.

"From the expression on your face, I take it you were not one of his staunch supporters."

Caroline nodded, before formulating an answer that would be politically correct. "He was a business man. A wheeler-dealer, so to say. Either you were for him above all others or you were not. He wanted to close our borders and for me and my husband it was like a slap in the face.

"Although my husband's grandparents were of English descent, his father was born in China. They adopted him as an infant and brought him to this country. His mother was white, making him half Chinese.

"As for me, I could trace my family not only to the European settlers who came here just after the Civil War, but also to one of the Native American tribes that inhabited the northern mid-west. The thought of immigration not being acceptable did not sit well with either one of us."

"May I ask why you opted to submit to suspended animation rather than fight for what you felt was important?"

Caroline laughed at his question. "You have no idea what things were like once the pandemic swept over the world. I saw only the beginning of it, but I had a premonition about what was to come and I wasn't strong enough to try to live through it. My husband was in China on a business trip when it first surfaced and he was one of the first Americans to die there. I thought my world ended the minute I learned of my husband's death. After that, all hell broke loose. Flights from China were banned and people who were on cruises all over the world had a hard time getting back home. All I could think of was what Hitler did to Europe in the 1930s and 1940s. I didn't want to live in a world like that. I decided it was for the best if I went to sleep for fifty years. If I was able to awaken, I prayed the world would be a better place than the one I was leaving."

The expression on President Addison's face was one of bewilderment. "Hitler?" he finally questioned.

The one-word inquiry confirmed what she'd been told for the past several days.

"What was a Hitler?"

"Who, not what. He was a horrible dictator who took over Germany and much of Europe before and during the second world war. He saw the Jews, as well as the Gypsies, as inferior and ordered their elimination. It was a horrible time in history. He put them into concentration camps and sent them to the ovens to be gassed and then burned alive. There were also mass shootings, where the people were lined up in front of deep pits that would become their graves once they were shot in the back."

"I-I didn't know. I've been told that history had been changed, but I never expected to hear anything like this. I have a feeling this meeting will have to be extended to many days, rather than a few hours. Another thing you mentioned was the Civil War. I was taught it was hardly more than a skirmish, you know, over almost before it started."

Caroline could feel tears welling in her eyes. "Since coming here, I've been studying some of the history books used in the schools. There is so much that has been left out, I am terrified as to what message we are sending to the next generations. How can anyone learn from the mistakes of the past if they do not know of them?"

President Addison ran his fingers through his hair. It was evident he was distraught by the minute information she'd just given him. Then and there she knew this was going to be a long and drawn out meeting. She prayed she would be able to fill in the gaps that were apparently missing in his knowledge of U.S. and world history.

Precisely at noon, an intimate meal was served for the two of them. Not having eaten much for breakfast, she realized just how hungry she was. She was delighted when they were served a stir-fry of chicken and fresh vegetables on a bed of white rice. She loved the Chinese/American flare of the meal and was surprised when the president ate his portion with great relish.

"It looks like we are going to be meeting for quite some time, Ms. Lewis," he said. "I would appreciate it if you would call me Brian, if I may call you Caroline."

"I have no problem with you calling me by my given name, but wouldn't it be inappropriate for me to call you by yours?"

"It would be, if I told you to. I'm not entirely comfortable with the title of President. I do know enough history to know that in the past there were two primary parties who ran the country. It wasn't long after you went into the state of suspended animation that things changed. People were tired of the rhetoric of both parties and decided to vote not for the party but for the candidate. I ran for the office because I wanted to make a difference in the world. I think there were a lot of people who were surprised when I won. No one had ever heard of me before, even though I had served in my state assembly before being elected. I am very interested in gleaning all the knowledge you have to impart to me. I want this country to go back to the values set up by the founding fathers."

Considering Brian's lack of knowledge for most history, his reference to the founding fathers and the values they set up caught her unawares. "I'm surprised people even remember the founding fathers, to say nothing of their values. I was afraid the Constitution as well as the Declaration of Independence have been forgotten along with so much of the history of this county."

"Those things were coming when the candidates, like me, decided we needed new leadership in our country. The first of these candidates surfaced in 2024 and were elected to national offices. By 2036 the first of these candidates was elected as President. Unfortunately, the damage had been done and history had been rewritten."

Caroline nodded. She understood exactly what Brian was saying. In 2020, change needed to happen, but she'd been uncertain as to which candidate she would have voted for. Thank goodness the change finally came, but not before the history of the world had been either rewritten or completely eradicated.

~ * ~

By dinner time, Caroline was completely exhausted. She'd hardly scratched the surface of the history of the United States for the late twentieth and early twenty-first centuries. There was so much more history that Brian knew nothing about. She wondered if it would be the same when she talked with leaders from the other countries.

Again, dinner was served in the elegant dining room. Since Tom and Nora had returned to Chicago over the weekend, their places at the table were taken by Brian and his aide. Once the introductions were made around the table, the meal, which she decided must resemble a state dinner at the White House, was served.

Aaron had been waiting for her outside of the dining room and graciously escorted her to her seat at the table. When Brian seated himself on the other side of her, she was surprised to see a glint of jealousy in Aaron's eyes.

How could he be jealous of the President of the United States? From what she'd learned, Brian had been happily married for over fifteen years and was the father of two small children.

The table conversation stayed light. She was glad the reason for Brian's visit to the facility was not brought up. Her head was so full of everything they'd discussed throughout the day, she had no desire to repeat any of it at dinner.

With dinner ended, Aaron escorted Caroline to her condo. "I couldn't believe you called the President of the United States by his first name," he finally said.

"It bothered me at first, but since we will be working so closely together over the next few days, he insisted we should be on a first-name basis. If I didn't know better, I'd say you were jealous."

"It wouldn't be hard to be jealous of you with anyone other than me. You have to admit you're a very beautiful woman. I'm certain there are many men who would be more than willing to have you interested in them."

"You seem to forget, I'm not interested in them. Besides, Brian is happily married. While we were eating lunch, he showed me pictures of his wife and kids. I think he's a very devoted husband."

"That's a relief. You will never know how pleased I am when you're with me. After my wife's passing, I thought I'd never love again. I know I haven't said it before, but I've fallen in love with you."

Aaron's proclamation of love brought a smile to Caroline's lips. Like Aaron, she thought love was a word she would never say again. Adam had been her husband, her soulmate and her best friend. As far as she was concerned, love was something she would never experience again. With her awakening in the twenty-second century she was given a second chance. Granted, Aaron was the exact opposite of Adam.

Although they'd traveled extensively and often went to the theatre, Adam always said while others worked to live, he lived to work. She worked beside him, but there were never the spontaneous dates and outings she experienced with Aaron.

Looking deep into Aaron's eyes, she honestly said, "I love you, too. I never thought there would be anyone other than Adam who would love me. I should discourage your attentions since chronologically I'm almost one hundred years older than you, but I feel no different now than when I went to sleep. I'm a forty-three-year-old woman who needs to be loved."

Aaron gave her a brilliant smile, before pulling her into an embrace. Without words between them, he kissed her, awakening all the senses she thought would never be awakened again.

Chapter Seventeen

Over the next several weeks, the proclamation of Caroline and Aaron's love for each other seemed to take a backseat to the other events going on around them.

Caroline became the center of attention for everyone at the complex. Dignitaries from all over the world visited and listened to the history she either remembered from personal experience or recalled from the studies she'd done in college.

The only time Caroline and Aaron met was at the official dinners that were meant to host the heads of state from countries in North and South America as well as Africa, Australia, Europe, Asia, and Antarctica.

The people who most intrigued her were those from Antarctica. She learned there were three different colonies of aliens living under the ice cap. From them, she learned of their visitations to various areas of the world, enabling them with the knowledge of written language, science, mathematics and medicine.

By evening, when she attended the dinners prepared for their honored guests, she found she was exhausted. Although she would have preferred quiet dinners with Aaron, she knew she was the link between these dignitaries and the earthly community. Her presence was expected, no matter how exhausting the day had been.

One of her favorite encounters was with the Prime Minister of England. She was an intelligent woman who was very interested in the information Caroline could give her regarding the history of her own country. It came as a surprise that the powers that be had erased the history of England in the same way as it had in the United States.

"How did England survive the natural disasters that hit both the east and west coasts of the United States?" Caroline inquired.

"It was miraculous, considering the damage done to France, Scandinavia and the Iberian Peninsula. It was as if the tsunami went completely around us. No one can understand how it happened. When it did, it brought many people back to God and the church. If you ask me it was a good thing, bad for the people on the continent but good for those of us that were missed. Bringing us back to God was a blessing."

Caroline nodded. Bringing people back to God was a good thing, but at what cost? From what she'd learned about the destruction on the east and west coasts of the U.S., she could only envision what happened to other countries around the world.

"Someday, perhaps, I can travel to the other continents of the world. I traveled a lot when I was first married back in the late twentieth century. To be truthful, we went to all seven continents."

"You must have been quite wealthy," the Prime Minister observed.

"My husband's family was well off, therefore, we were as well. His parents owned a chain of Chinese/American restaurants, which we inherited when they passed away. We managed them for several years along with running an internet-based business. He was on a buying trip in China when the pandemic first hit. I guess that's why I'm here today. I felt as though I couldn't live without him."

"Like our country being saved from destruction, I have a feeling your decision to have your body put into a state of suspended animation was divine intervention."

Caroline didn't know if she totally agreed with the Prime Minister. From what she'd been told by Cassion and Hodia, it was entirely possible that her life had been spared by the aliens who had been monitoring planet Earth for many years.

~ * ~

"To what do I owe the honor of your presence?" Caroline asked

Hodia, when she appeared at the condo with a breakfast tray.

"I am here on official business. I also thought you would enjoy having breakfast with me. I even brought mimosas."

"What kind of official business? Since I have been meeting with the world leaders, I haven't seen you, Cassion or Dr. Aragon."

"I'm here on behalf of the contingency from Antarctica. They would like to extend an invitation for you and Aaron to come to tour their bases under the ice cap. Is this something that might be of interest to you?"

Caroline's mind spun at the prospect of seeing something that had been nothing more than speculation before she went into suspended animation.

"I've always loved to travel. Back in the early twenty-first century, my husband and I took a cruise to Antarctica. I stepped foot on the continent with no knowledge of what lay beneath the surface. I would be thrilled to be able to explore that which no one knew existed when I was last there. What does Aaron say about taking this trip?"

"I wanted to talk to you before I broached the subject with him."

"Perhaps that is for the best. Although we professed our love for each other weeks ago, I've been so busy we've had very little time for personal conversation. I don't even know what he's been doing with his time."

"I can answer that," Hodia said. "With his library skills he has been invaluable in cataloging the many books we have rescued since they have been discovered by the archaeology teams working on both the east and west coasts of the United States. I have been delighted with the copies of Shakespeare, as well as Dickens, that he found in the many boxes from the various digs. Up until now, we have had no one with the skills to catalog all of these volumes. He has been a godsend. None of us had any idea what to do with written books. For centuries we have read books digitally and not anything written by the writers of Earth, especially those that are considered to be masters of their craft."

"I'm pleased to think he has been of help to you and your contemporaries. I worried about him becoming bored with being here only because of me."

Hodia took a sip of her mimosa seemingly collecting her thoughts. "Since you have no scheduled meetings, may I suggest the two of you take a day of leisure to discuss the trip we are proposing?"

Caroline agreed and thanked her friend for giving her the opportunity to broach the subject of the proposed trip to previously unexplored lands.

~ * ~

Caroline felt as nervous as a schoolgirl as she stood outside the door to Aaron's condo. Before she could ring the bell, the door opened. If he was surprised to see her, he didn't show it.

"You look beautiful this morning," he greeted her.

"Why, thank you, kind sir. I've been told that both of us have a day off. I was hoping we could spend it together."

"Do I have to ask just who told you this?"

"Hodia came and we shared breakfast."

Aaron laughed at her statement. "I had breakfast brought to me this morning by Cassion. He mentioned a trip to Antarctica and was hoping I could talk you into going with me."

Now it was Caroline's turn to laugh. "I was asked to talk you into going with me. How do you feel about such a trip? I have met the dignitaries from the major groups with complexes under the ice cap and found them all to be very amenable. Having been to Antarctica when I thought of it as only a place of bone-chilling cold and penguins, I'm excited to see what the world under the ice cap looks like."

"It sounds like we're both on the same page with this. For today, how would you like to go exploring? I have finally had my personal hover craft delivered and we could take a picnic lunch to Pike's Peak. Have you been there before?"

"Of all the traveling Adam and I did, very little of it was done within the continental United States. I loved traveling the world, but I didn't actually explore my own country. I have a feeling there could be some good hiking there, but I'd rather enjoy the landscape. I'll go home and change into something more suitable to traveling. Can you pick me up in about a half an hour?"

"I'm ready to go now. Cassion provided me with a pre-packed lunch. I'll walk you back to your place and we can leave from there. I don't want to miss a minute of being with you."

Caroline loved the idea of Aaron taking her home. She'd missed his company over the past weeks.

~ * ~

Caroline marveled at the panorama that played out before her as they flew from the complex toward the Rocky Mountains. No matter what natural disasters hit the coasts of the United States, these magnificent mountains stood in all their majesty as they had stood since the beginning of time.

Once they landed at Pike's Peak, Aaron helped her get out of the craft before escorting her to one of the many scenic lookout points.

"We need to talk about this trip to Antarctica," he said, once they were seated on one of the benches provided for the tourists.

"What is there to talk about? I think this is an excellent opportunity for both of us."

"I couldn't agree more. I'm also looking forward to having some alone time for the two of us, but there is something that I'd like to address before we leave. You know I was married for many years. I also know you and Adam shared a loving relationship. When I lost my wife, I never thought the day would come then I would find someone I loved as much as I did her. Our meeting was something that threw me for a loop. When I realized you loved me as much as I loved you, I knew I wanted you in my life for as long as the Good Lord sees fit to allow us to be together. What I'm trying to say is, will you do me the honor of becoming my wife before we leave for Antarctica?"

Caroline gasped with delight. "I-I don't know what to say. On second thought, I do know what to say. Yes, how soon do you think we can get all of the arrangements made?"

"Hopefully we can do this at warp speed, since Cassion says he wants to plan the trip to Antarctica for the first week of next month. Do you think you can be ready so quickly?"

"I would like to have Tom and Nora with us. Of course, I'm certain they can arrange to come here if we contact them immediately with our plans. Considering Kirsten was the first member of the family I met when I awakened, I'd like her to be my maid of honor. Do you know who you would like to have as your best man.?"

"I called Tom as soon as I heard about this trip. Him being your closest male relative and a good friend of mine for many years, I asked him for his blessing as well as if he would be my best man. He said he thought it was about time I came to my senses and asked you to marry me. Cassion said we could probably have everything ready in less than a week. There is a minister at the complex and..."

Caroline leaned over and kissed him, mid-sentence. "I love the fact that you've covered all your bases, so to say, but did anyone ever tell you, you talk too much?"

Their embrace tightened, bringing stares and nervous laughter from the other tourists who were enjoying the scenic views before beginning the assent to the top of Pike's Peak.

At last, they broke apart and Aaron pulled a jewelry box from his pocket. Inside was a beautiful diamond ring set with a ruby on one side and an emerald on the other.

"The diamond is a sign of my undying love, the ruby is my birthstone and the emerald is your birthstone."

"It's beautiful," Caroline gasped. "How long have you been planning this?"

"Ever since the night you told me you loved me as much as I loved you. When we saw so little of each other these past few weeks, I worried perhaps you had changed your mind. This morning, after meeting with Cassion, I knew I couldn't agree to the trip unless we were married."

~ * ~

As soon as they returned to the complex, Caroline sent a message to Kirsten asking her to join her for the evening meal. Once assured both Kirsten and Kevin would be joining them for dinner, they went to meet with Pastor David, the minister of the church within the complex.

"Cassion told me you would be coming to see me today," Pastor David greeted them. "I assume you are here to discuss wedding plans. How soon do you want to have the ceremony?"

"I know it's quick, but we're leaving for Antarctica in about three weeks and we'd like to be married before we depart. Since today is Friday, do you think we can be married two weeks from tomorrow?"

Caroline smiled at the way Aaron took charge of the situation. He was getting right to the point and setting in motion the hurried wedding.

From the pastor's office, Caroline insisted on going shopping for her bridal gown on her own. Buried deeply in her memories were the old warnings about the groom not seeing the bride in her bridal gown before the day of the wedding.

Looking through the various pictures of wedding gowns, she chose a floor-length sheath in a delicate blush pink. It was overlaid with sheer lace and was strapless. Caroline thought it was the most beautiful dress she'd ever seen. After taking her measurements, the sales associate assured her it would be ready for her by the end of the coming week. There would be plenty of time for any adjustments that needed to be made.

By the time Caroline returned to her condo, Aaron, Kirsten and Kevin were waiting for her.

"I've made reservations at one of the restaurants in the complex. They are for seven, so you do have time to freshen up before we have to leave."

She agreed, she did want to freshen up. While Kevin and Aaron waited in the living room of the condo, Kirsten went with her to the bedroom to pick an appropriate gown for this evening's meal.

"Oh, Aunt Caroline, this is the most exciting thing I can think of. I can't believe you were able to get everything planned so quickly."

"I know. It's been quite overwhelming. This morning all I could think of was taking a trip to Antarctica to tour the facilities under the ice cap. Now, I'm in the midst of planning a wedding. I hope you will agree to being my maid of honor."

"I'll be thrilled. Aaron told me that my dad is going to be his best man. Do you have any idea what you want me to wear?"

Caroline reached into her purse and produced the picture of the gown she'd chosen for Kirsten. "Since my gown is blush pink, I'd like yours to be of a deeper shade of pink. If that meets with your approval, you'll need to contact the seamstress with your measurements so the dress will fit you perfectly."

Kirsten studied the picture of the dress Caroline chose for her. The style was one she would have chosen for herself. Like Caroline's dress, it was a strapless sheath with a sheer jacket of a lighter pink, but one that was still darker than the gown Caroline would wear.

"It's beautiful. I know exactly where the seamstress's shop is. It's not far from the hospital and since I'm working on Monday, I'll be able to drop by there on my lunch hour. Are you sure they can have the dresses ready on time?"

"They assured me I can stop in for a fitting a week from today. It's entirely possible yours can be done by then as well."

Caroline left Kirsten sitting in the bedroom while she took a refreshing shower and applied her makeup. By the time she returned to the bedroom, Kirsten picked out the perfect dress for their evening out.

~ * ~

The restaurant Aaron chose was in an upscale neighborhood not far from the complex. As soon as they arrived, they were enthusiastically greeted by the owner. He personally escorted them to their table.

"I have everything you ordered, sir," he said, addressing Aaron.

A chilled bottle of champagne waited for them, as well as an appetizer platter. On the platter were oysters on the half shell, deep fried mushrooms, onion rings, cheese curds and spinach artichoke dip with chips for dipping.

"If we eat all of this, we won't have room for the main course," Caroline teased.

"I hope you have room, "Aaron replied. "I've ordered prime rib of buffalo with loaded baked potatoes and chocolate mousse for dessert."

"Thank goodness all of those things are calorie free. If they weren't, I'd never fit into the dress that I ordered for our wedding this afternoon."

Caroline had to admit that everything Aaron ordered was delicious.

She'd never had buffalo before and was pleasantly surprised by the taste and texture of the meat. "I'd heard about people who bred buffalo for meat back in the early twenty-first century, but I never had the pleasure to try it before. This is wonderful."

"I have a friend in Wisconsin who runs one of the breeding farms. He told me that his son was moving out here to start a similar operation. He's a partner in this restaurant. When you were busy with the state dinners, I decided to come and see if the quality was as good as what was served at the restaurant in Wisconsin. I certainly wasn't disappointed. I knew it would be the perfect place for us to celebrate our engagement."

"I applaud you on your choice," Kevin said, raising his glass in a toast. "I will certainly remember this place when I find a special lady I want to impress."

Chapter Eighteen

The morning of the wedding dawned with a brilliant October sun shining in a clear blue sky. Tom and Nora arrived two days earlier and now Nora fussed over the dresses for both Caroline and Kirsten.

"This is such a glorious day," Nora declared, once everyone was ready for the service to begin. "Tom and I are so excited to think the two of you are getting married."

"I totally agree," Caroline replied. "I never thought there would be a man who could measure up to Adam, but Aaron makes me complete."

Together, the three of them walked to the garden of the church where they would be exchanging their vows. The outdoor service had been Caroline's idea. Even with the unpredictable weather, she prayed this day would be perfect. Just in case, she knew she could have moved everything into the chapel.

She waited just out of sight as Kirsten started her walk toward the altar to be met by her father. Once she took her place, Kevin held out his arm. "Are you ready for this, Aunt Caroline?" he whispered.

"I feel just as nervous as I did on the day of my first wedding. I was just twenty-three on that day. I can't believe I'm just twenty years older, even though it's been one hundred and twenty years in the past."

The music changed and Caroline began the walk to take her to Aaron's side. As soon as she entered his line of vision, she saw him begin to smile.

This is the right decision for you, my love, Adam's voice sounded in her head.

How can this be? she silently questioned.

I have been with you ever since you awakened. God has allowed me to become your guardian spirit. Aaron is the perfect man to make your life complete. I am only saddened that it took a hundred years for you to find him. Be happy, my love. My work is done.

She could feel tears prickle behind her eyelids but willed them not to fall. Today was the first day of her new life and Adam's blessing attested to it.

~ * ~

Aaron stood at the altar awaiting Caroline's appearance. As soon as he saw her, he was in awe. The color of her gown was perfect for her coloring. He thought for a moment she was one of the angels that were depicted in the stained-glass windows of the church that sat as a backdrop for their outdoor wedding.

He was surprised when she had a faraway look in her eyes. It was as though she was carrying on a conversation with an unseen entity. The moment passed and her brilliant smile replaced the earlier look he'd seen.

It seemed to take an eternity for her to complete the walk to stand by his side. He held out his hand to her. After handing her bouquet to Kirsten, she took his hand in hers.

"Who gives this woman to this man?" the pastor asked.

"On behalf of my family I am pleased to present Aunt Caroline to the man who will now become my uncle," Kevin said.

For Aaron, the remainder of the service was a blur. He knew what the vows would be, but he knew in the future he would never remember them. All he could see and think about was this beautiful woman who had agreed to make him one of the happiest men in the world.

~ * ~

The restaurant where they officially announced their engagement catered the reception. Although there weren't many people there, the people they'd met and worked with at the complex were honored guests.

"When we first met you, we never thought we would be witnessing your wedding," Cassion said, as he shook hands with Aaron and kissed Caroline's cheek.

"I hope you approve," Caroline replied.

"More than approve," Hodia commented. "I always cry at weddings, but today I smiled uncontrollably. This was definitely a wedding made in heaven and ordained by the One God."

"I think you're right," Caroline agreed. "Just before I started down the aisle, my first husband's voice sounded in my head. He said God sent him to watch over me since I awakened so many months ago. I never thought I would have a guardian angel, but I guess God had a different idea."

With the reception finished, Caroline and Aaron went to the hotel at the space port to spend the night before their flight, which would be leaving the next day for the underground bases in Antarcticia.

Chapter Nineteen

Caroline strapped herself into the seat of the craft prior to take-off. Beside her, Aaron clasped his seatbelt before taking her hand in his.

"I never thought I would be taking off on such a wonderful adventure," he said. "You told me you've been to Antarctica. What do you remember of it?"

"I remember it was very cold and everything was blindingly white. We were on a cruise that left from Brazil. We had stops at several ports of call along the South American coast, including Patagonia. When I first saw the seventh continent I was in awe. Thankfully, Adam insisted I wear a heavy parka. We weren't on the continent very long because it was so cold; we were anxious to get back to our warm stateroom. Before that we'd been on six continents and this was something we both wanted to do. Little did I know what lay beneath the ice and snow."

"Do you think we'll be landing on the surface of the continent?"

"From what I've been told by the dignitaries I've been meeting with, we will descend through one of the volcanos to land at the space port that is located in the middle of the area between the three different settlements that have been established there. I'm certain we will see similarities to the complex in Colorado, but at the same time I have a feeling it will be more futuristic than either of us can imagine."

The flight took off as smoothly as any of the other flights she'd been on since returning from the simulated sleep of suspended animation. This would be the longest flight she'd been on and she was surprised when they were told they could move around the cabin.

Since Cassion and Hodia were taking the trip with them, they met them in the dining area of the ship. "Our luncheon will be served soon. Before we settle down to eat, perhaps you would like to see your quarters. Because this is an overnight flight, we have all been assigned sleeping quarters."

"I don't know if I will be able to sleep," Aaron replied to Cassion's comment. "I'm so excited about where we are going and what we are going to see, sleep could be a stranger."

"I doubt that," Hodia said. "In a couple of hours, the boredom of travel will give way to the need for sleep. You'll need it, since tomorrow will be a very busy day, filled not only with landing at the space port but also the official tours you will be making during this visit."

~ * ~

Caroline was surprised at how refreshed she felt when she awakened the next morning. Although she thought sleep would be a stranger, she knew she must have fallen asleep the minute her head hit the pillow.

After brushing her teeth and doing her morning clean up, she joined Cassion and Hodia in the dining area for the morning meal.

"If you look out the window, you will see we are approaching Antarcticia," Hodia advised them. "This is such a spectacular view, it is something I don't want you to miss."

Caroline looked out the window, she expected to see the rugged coastline she remembered from the cruise she'd taken with Adam over a century earlier. Instead, the aerial view showed a much different panorama. Before them loomed a powerful volcano.

"That is our destination," Cassion said. "Our ancestors found this gateway to the underworld. You will be surprised by the paradise they have founded beneath this cap of ice and snow. It is said that the original explorers left this land once the snow began to fall and did not stop. Little did they know that beneath the ice cap there was still the paradise they first found here. I am certain both of you will be impressed."

Caroline gasped as the hover craft began to make the descent into the mouth of the waiting volcano. For a moment fear overtook her excitement. What would she find? Would she be impressed as Cassion said, or would she be overwhelmed? Was this a trap or the gateway to paradise?

From outside the cabin, artificial light, produced by the thermal energy provided by the volcano, illuminated the cabin. She could feel her eyes widen with wonder as she saw the trees and flowering plants that surrounded the space port.

"How is this possible? We just descended through a volcano. Where is the molten lava I've heard can spew forth, destroying everything within its path?" Caroline inquired.

"The magma is still beneath us, but long ago our ancestors learned how to harness its power to illuminate this paradise as well as grow the vegetables, trees and flowers you will soon be seeing for yourself."

"Why keep this knowledge to yourselves?" Aaron asked.

"We had to wait until the time was right for us to make our presence known. As for our advanced technologies, the population of earth is not ready for such advanced knowledge."

"Then why show this to us?" Caroline persisted.

"You are from the past and Aaron is a man of knowledge. It will be with your cooperation that we will be able to help the population of Earth to learn these new ways of life. This will be a boon for everyone. In the past we have had to be content to advisors only. You, Caroline, are what is being touted as a National Treasure. Once you tell the people about the advances we have made, volcanos all over the world will be harnessed for the good of the people. We can turn this planet into the virtual paradise the One God planned for it to be before the beginning of time."

Caroline contemplated the impact of Cassion's words. Was a paradise what the world was like when it was created? Was the Garden of Eden an apt description of what the world was like or was it merely a fantasy portrayed to…to what? She didn't know. Had the world changed with the ice age, or Noah's flood?

"I know what the Bible tells me about the creation of the world.

Have I been deceiving myself all these years?"

"No, Caroline, you have not been deceived. The One God did create the world, the world that was a paradise. He also destroyed much of what he had built both by the ice age and the great flood. There were humanoid people here when the first aliens arrived. They were the hunter-gatherers who were quick to learn the ways of the One God. He has spent eons cultivating the people who live here to become the intelligent individuals you are. The time is now right to complete the education of the population of the world."

The time is now right. Those words echoed in the confines of her mind. She never thought of herself as someone who could help mankind make the transition to a new way of life.

~ * ~

The craft landed and to Caroline's surprise, they were met by the three dignitaries she'd met with weeks earlier. The first was Dr. Gratan, the second, Prime Minister Kalos, and the third Senator Drago.

"I'm overwhelmed," she said, after accepting their greetings. "I had no idea our arrival in your provinces would garner such a prestigious greeting. I am truly honored and look forward to touring your magnificent communities."

"It is we who are honored to have you as our guest. The time is right for the world to be enlightened. After meeting with you, as well as Aaron, we feel the time is right and the two of you are the best people to help us enlighten the people of Earth."

They were escorted to their accommodations. Once they were settled, they were summoned to the state building where they were greeted by many more dignitaries and professional people.

"Recently, I was kidnaped by the militant agents, or at least I thought they were militant agents, in order for them to find where Caroline had been taken," Aaron said. "My first and most important job in life is to protect the woman I love. Can you say the same thing? Will you be able to protect Caroline as well as myself from the people who want the truth to be stifled? I didn't realize how much of history had been erased by the powers that be, until I met Caroline. From what I can see, she is a threat to not only the United States but also the world."

Caroline was astounded by Aaron's statement. Although she'd asked him what occurred during his incarceration, he'd refused to talk to her about it. "What happened to you when…"

"You can say it, Caroline, when I was taken by the people who wanted to do you harm. I don't think they were sent by the government, but by a militant group intent on defacing the Earth with the lies that have been circulated for more than a century. It is time for the truth to be known, and for all of us gathered here to show this world the beauty of the future."

From around the table, the dignitaries, as well as the professional people, congratulated Aaron for his insight and determination.

Caroline was just as impressed as the others. Admittedly, she loved Aaron for the man she met. Today she loved him more for the man who would be her partner in life. Together it was entirely possible they could change the world for the better.

~ * ~

In the days that followed, Caroline and Aaron were shown the wonders that the underground provinces had to offer.

"I could live here," she commented, once they were back at their hotel. "This is the most beautiful place I've ever seen. It's truly the Garden of Eden."

"It certainly is, but you seem to forget why we were brought here. The world has to know what the militant groups have done to history. I know you spoke with many of the world's leaders, but how many of them actually listened to and agreed with what you had to tell them? The job we have to do is a big one and I think together we can handle it, but not if we stay here. We have to return to Denver and work through people like Cassion and Hodia to enlighten the world."

Caroline nodded her agreement. "I know we do. Living here is little more than a pipe dream. We'll be meeting with the leaders again in the morning. We can give them our decision about staying at that time. Hopefully, we will be allowed to return here when we're in need of a vacation."

Chapter Twenty

The trip back to Colorado mirrored the trip they'd taken to Antarctica days earlier. They left just prior to the evening meal. This time, she questioned Hodia about the possibility of the food being drugged to ensure them a good night's sleep while on the craft.

"You are very perceptive. This is a practice we have used on all of our long flights to ensure proper rest. We are no different from you. We find that excitement over what is to come tends to keep sleep at bay. It is easier to mix a mild sedative with the food than to become too apprehensive and not get the appropriate rest needed."

"That makes sense," Caroline agreed. "I wish I'd known about it on our first flight. Of course, I did appreciate getting such a good night's sleep before we landed. You were right it was a busy and trying time."

While they ate, Hodia and Cassion turned the conversation to the future. "How do you propose we proceed when we return to the complex?"

Caroline was at a loss for words, but Aaron was not. "I think we should be very careful in how we undertake the changes that will be necessary. I met with President Addison and I feel he will be a great ally, but there are groups out there who do not want history to be known, to say nothing of repeated. It's those groups who are the enemy we will have to fight. I'm not certain if we can handle this alone. What do you suggest?"

Cassion didn't answer immediately. "While you were being introduced to our society, Hodia and I were in talks with Dr. Gratan, Prime Minister Kalos and Senator Drago. They agree this is something the four of us cannot accomplish alone. They are putting together a task force that will arrive at the complex within the next month. Those who will be coming are of the most qualified men and women in the field of diplomacy as well as historians."

Caroline was relieved. Although she was well versed in the history of Earth, both that which happened within her lifetime but also what she'd learned while majoring in history in college, she knew she wasn't equipped to take on the groups of militants who didn't want the history of the world known.

~ * ~

Dr. Gratan led the task force that arrived at the complex within three weeks of Caroline and Aaron's return. He brought with him six men and six women who were experts in their fields of communication and governmental issues.

They attended several strategy meetings before they finally agreed to make a public announcement of the reinstatement of the history of not only the nation but also the world.

Television cameras and reporters were gathered in the meeting space within the complex. "Good Evening," the commentator greeted the viewing audience.

"Today it is our pleasure to introduce Aaron Phillips, his wife Caroline Lewis-Phillips, and Dr. Gratan, along with his task force from the provinces of Antarctica. I turn the platform over to Ms. Lewis-Philips."

Caroline got to her feet, still feeling apprehensive but better prepared than she would have been without Dr. Gratan's assistance.

"Thank you," she said into the micophone. "Several months ago, I made the headlines by returning from the dead. Over a hundred years ago I opted to go into suspended animation rather than face the horrors of the pandemic that I have now learned took over the entire planet. Once I returned, I took a position at a Chicago area library. I subsequently learned how the history of our country as well as the world had been eradicated. Over the past months, I have worked with the leaders of many of the countries around the world, as well as representatives of the provinces that flourish beneath the ice cap of Antarctica.

"Today, I have agreed to do this interview in order to set the record straight as to what happened in our world before the groups who want this information to be suppressed can take steps to silence me."

She paused for a moment to contemplate her thoughts. "During my lifetime, I saw the Gulf War, 9/11, the wars in Afghanistan and Iraq, along with the rise and fall of ISIS. The last was the first I'd heard of the destruction of history. I was horrified when I realized that many of the ancient artifacts from the Middle East had been desecrated or destroyed.

"Since my return to life, one hundred years after I decided to go into the suspended animation, I've learned of the destruction not only of ancient artifacts but the facts surrounding all of history. Monuments have been torn down, wars like the Revolutionary War, the Civil War, World War I, World War II, the Korean Conflict and Vietnam trivialized.

"Over the past weeks, I have been honored to meet with Dr. Gratan and his team. It is our hope to set the records straight and reinstall our histories back in our minds and our classrooms."

Communicators within the room began to go off as messages came in, both pro and con to what she was saying. As she could have predicted, those who wanted history suppressed, voiced their concerns loud and clear.

She was surprised when a hologram of President Addison projected onto a screen of the conference room.

"I was going to use my communicator to comment on Caroline's speech. Unfortunately, all of the airwaves were jammed with other callers. I have personally met with her and was horrified when she told me things about the history of our country of which I had no idea. At the time, she told me that those who ignore history are destined to repeat it.

"Since returning to Washington, I have delved deeply into ancient history. Since most of it has been eradicated, I needed to go into the old databases. I found many movies from the twentieth century that depicted the history she spoke to me about. For the first time, I saw the horrors of the wars our country has been involved in since its fight for independence almost four hundred years ago. In my education, I'd read nothing about the slavery that was addressed by the Civil War of the middle nineteenth century nor the race riots of the twentieth and twenty-first centuries.

"I am signing into law a procuration saying our history can and will be restored, thanks to the tireless work of Caroline Lewis-Phillips, Aaron Phillips, Dr. Gratan and his team of experts."

As soon as his transmission ended, the communicators were again jammed with transmissions, many in favor of what he said, but the majority of them were protesters.

Once Caroline took her seat next to Aaron, he squeezed her hand reassuringly. "You were fabulous. It didn't hurt our cause to have Brian give us his support."

The experience left Caroline completely exhausted. Rather than answer Aaron, she leaned heavily against his shoulder. Whatever it was that Dr. Gratan and the rest of his team said didn't register. The only things she could think about were the ramifications that could come about because of what she'd said today.

~ * ~

Aaron was as worried as Caroline. He knew how he'd suffered at the hands of the militants, even though it had only been a matter of three days he'd been held in captivity. He'd only confided what happened to him to Cassion. It was best if Caroline never knew what he'd endured.

They were seated in the formal dining room for dinner, when Cassion came into the room. "I'm sorry to intrude, but we have put the entire compound on lockdown. There are armed protesters heading our way. The bulletproof shield has been activated. Until further notice, no one will be allowed to leave the compound for any reason."

"Oh dear, this is all my fault," Caroline lamented. "If I hadn't come back from the dead to report history as I remembered it, none of this would have happened."

"It's not your fault," Dr. Gratan consoled her. "I predicted this but made no mention of it to you before this. I was hopeful the protests of the past wouldn't be repeated, but I can see because history has been changed, no one knows the ramifications of violence in the past. We will weather this storm and possibly make sense to those who are protesting. If not, I'm afraid there will be open hostilities."

Caroline couldn't stop the tears that rolled down her cheeks. This was what she'd been told happened at the peak of the pandemic. Somehow, that information had been cataloged and kept by the aliens who populated the complex. It was too bad they hadn't been able to save more of the world's history.

Chapter Twenty-One

Although Caroline didn't actually see the protesters, she saw transmissions of them yelling, "History doesn't matter!"

"History does matter," she yelled at the communicator screen. "Why can't they see what they are doing? This is exactly what happened during the race riots of the twentieth and twenty-first centuries. By being ignorant of history, they are repeating it. I just pray no one will be injured or worse yet killed."

Aaron shook his head at her tirade. "Are you certain this was what it was like?"

"Positive. I wasn't born until the 1970s but my mother was born in the 50s. She told stories of when schools were first intergraded. I also learned about it in college. Firehoses and dogs were turned on the black people who were clamoring for the rights guaranteed to everyone in the Declaration of Independence for the United States. It wasn't just here, but I remember when refugees were pouring into Europe to escape the wars that were erupting in Africa and the Middle East. There were terrible protests and terrorist actions at that time as well."

The ringing of the doorbell interrupted Caroline's recounting of the history she remembered happening in her lifetime.

Aaron motioned for her to remain seated while he went to answer the door. She was surprised when Zora, one of the women who came with Dr. Gratan, entered the living room.

"I'm pleased to see you," Caroline said, getting to her feet.

"I am also pleased to see you, but don't get up on my account. Dr. Gratan sent me here to tell you about the talks that have been scheduled between our task force, you, Aaron and the protesters."

"Talks?" Aaron questioned.

"The state of Colorado sent a group from the National Guard to make certain the protests are peaceful. President Addison also sent people from Washington to talk to them. Between the troops and President Addison's representative, they have gotten the protesters to stand down. The leaders of their groups have agreed to meet with those of us who have been researching the lost history of this planet."

"When are these talks scheduled to be held?" Caroline asked.

"Tomorrow morning, in the conference room where you held the press conference."

"Will that be safe?"

Zora smiled. "You will be very safe. Not only will our security guards be there, but President Addison will be there along with representatives of the National Guard from Colorado. Your safety is of the upmost importance, not only to everyone within the complex, but people all over the globe."

Once Zora left, Caroline gave into her apprehension over the entire situation. "I don't have a good feeling about this meeting. What if these people have agreed to this only to be allowed entrance into the complex? Do you think we could be in danger?"

"I pray not, but only time will tell. For now, let's go out into the garden. We know there we will be safe and we can enjoy the beautiful weather, even though it is cold and snowing outside of the protective shield."

~ * ~

Early the next morning, security guards from the compound arrived to take Caroline and Aaron to the scheduled meeting in the conference room.

She was pleased to find Brian Addison waiting for them. "Are you sure you should be here?" she questioned, after greeting him.

"This disturbance is against the history of our nation. I would be a poor president if I stayed in Washington while civil unrest unfolded everywhere in the United States. There are secret service agents posted both inside and outside of the complex."

They only had to wait a few minutes for the leaders of the protesters to arrive. Caroline looked at the young men and marveled at how much they resembled the protesters she remembered from the early twenty-first century. Each of them had shaved their heads and they were dressed in what she would have called military fatigues with swastikas sown to the sleeves of their shirts.

At least the fashions of the militants haven't changed much in the last one hundred years, she thought. Even so, seeing the swastikas brought fear to her entire being. She vividly remembered reading of the atrocities carried out by Adolf Hitler in Europe during the second world war.

"We are here at the request of the government and the aliens," the young man, who introduced himself as Patrick Ernst greeted them. "We are against all of this ancient history crap. We are also against the aliens coming to take over our country. We recognize only the superior race."

"Hogwash," Caroline shouted. "This superior race you're talking about was a product of the mind of a sick individual known by the name of Adolf Hitler."

Patrick's expression changed from one of hatred to one of bewilderment. "Who are you talking about?"

"I'm talking about the man who first decided people who weren't white, blond and blue-eyed weren't worth living. I have a feeling, by looking at your beards, you aren't blonds and neither of you have blue eyes. Had you lived in Hitler's Germany, you might have been sent to a concentration camp, starved and possibly sent to the gas chamber. You are blessed to be able to live in a country where you are free to voice your opinion. The problem, as I see it, is with history and the monuments depicting it being eradicated, you have no idea what happened before you or even your parents were born. I suggest you, as well as your associates, take the time to read the bits and pieces of history that I have been able to fill in. I realize it's not complete by any stretch of the imagination, but once you know what price was paid for your freedom, you might understand what we are hoping to bring back to the people of Earth."

"Are you certain about this?"

Caroline could feel exasperation filling her mind and body. "I'm positive. Violence cures nothing whatsoever. How many of your people have you lost because of the violence you are perpetuating?"

The second young man, who identified himself as Christopher Laughlin, looked up at her with tears in his eyes. "I lost my two of my best friends. I thought it was because of the government and I wanted to fight them. Now I can see that I was wrong. Can you teach me about this history I haven't learned?"

Caroline held out her hand to Christopher. "I feel so sorry for the people of this generation who know nothing of history. I can fill in some of the gaps, but until a program of teaching what has been lost is instituted, it won't be complete. What you do need to know is that the aliens have come here to advise, rather than to rule. I have toured their home base under the ice cap of Antarctica and was extremely impressed. We have much to learn from these people, but first and foremost we much learn from the past."

"I heard you talk of race riots," Patrick said. "What were they?"

"Let me answer this one," Aaron replied. "Since I've met my wife, I've done extensive research. In the early days of our country, black people were kidnapped from their homes in Africa and brought here as slaves. Even when they were freed, they were still looked upon as second-class citizens. For many years it was white versus black. Over history, other people have been discriminated against. Be they Irish, German, Oriental, Hispanic, black, white, red or yellow, we are all created equal. Even the Native Americans who were here before any of the other settlers arrived were persecuted and many of them were wiped out. There is no superior race, just narrow-minded prejudice."

The remainder of the meeting was a back and forth between Dr. Gratan, President Addison, Patrick and Christopher. Caroline knew her presence wasn't necessary but she was pleased to be included.

At noon, a luncheon was served and while they were eating,

Christopher requested a private meeting with Caroline. Although everyone was concerned about the request, she assured them she would be perfectly safe.

~ * ~

While Patrick and the others remained in the conference room, a security officer led Caroline and Christopher into a private meeting room.

"Thank you for agreeing to meet with me privately," he said, once they were seated on two of the overstuffed chairs. "I have some questions and I didn't want to ask them in front of Patrick."

"I can understand your need for privacy. What is it you want to know?"

Christopher ran his hand over his shaved head, as though he remembered what it had been like to have a full head of hair.

"I don't know anything about my family. I was brought up in an orphanage, because both of my parents were killed in a hovercraft accident on their way to the hospital to give birth to me. My father was killed instantly and my mother lived long enough for the doctors to deliver me by caesarian section. They didn't have any identification, so the authorities didn't know who to call. I was taken immediately to a ranch for unwanted boys. I was told that because my DNA showed I was Native American, it was impossible for them to place me for adoption. I never knew what that meant and no one at the orphanage could tell me anything about it.

"Don't get me wrong, I thought I had a good experience at the Henderson Ranch. There never seemed to be enough to eat, and the punishments were harsh. Still, we lived on a ranch and were able to ride horses as well as work with the cattle. Even so, I wanted to know what it was like to have a family. When I turned eighteen, I aged out of the program. I met up with Patrick and the others. For the first time I had people who cared about me, because I was me. No one knew about the stigma that kept me from being adopted. I was ashamed of it, more because I had no idea what it means, than for who I was.

"I heard your husband mention atrocities done against the Native Americans, but who were they?"

Caroline wiped tears from her eyes. Like so much of history, the first citizens of this country had been forgotten, or maybe they'd been eradicated, just as the military in the nineteenth century wanted.

"I guess I should start at the beginning. First I would like to know if your DNA denoted the identity of the tribe you're associated with."

Christopher reached into the pocket of his pants and pulled out a piece of paper. "This is what I was given when Mr. Henderson told me I had to leave. I didn't know what any of it meant."

"Are you telling me you don't know how to read?"

Christopher shook his head. "I was told I was a nobody. My name was given to me by the doctor who delivered me. I was told I was so premature they didn't think I would survive the night after I was born. I guess I beat the odds. Anyway, Mr. Henderson didn't think education was a top priority. Those of us who were deemed unadoptable were taught a trade. My trade was a carpenter or a rancher. I wasn't as good at ranching as most of the kids. Of course, there wasn't much call for someone like me when I aged out. I was lucky to find Patrick and the others."

Caroline scanned the paper Christopher gave her. "It says here you have European ancestry as well as Cheyenne heritage. The Cheyenne were here along with the other tribes that populated this country before the white man came to take their land as well as their lives. When I did my Native American studies, the Cheyenne were the ones who were the most interesting to me. If you would like to learn more about them, I would be honored to teach you not only about your ancestors but also how to read and write. Of course, that would mean you would have to leave Patrick's group and come to live here at the complex. I know there are many others here who would be excellent teachers for you."

A worried expression crossed Christopher's face. "I don't know how Patrick and the others would feel about me leaving them to come to live here."

"Why don't we just sit quietly for a while and pray on it?" Caroline suggested.

"Pray? What is that?"

With that one question, Caroline broke down in tears. How could this young man have grown up ignorant and with no knowledge of God? With her communicator, she typed a message to Hodia and asked her to join them. Perhaps the two of them could work together to convince this young man he needed to join them for the education, heritage and love of God he'd been deprived of whilst growing up.

Hodia arrived within minutes of Caroline's message. Christopher was still sitting quietly. Caroline knew he was contemplating the option Caroline posed to him.

"I'm Hodia," she said as she entered the room. "I'm told you are Christopher."

The young man looked up, the last hint of any earlier tears still glinting in his eyes. "You're one of the aliens who want to take over our planet, aren't you?"

"I am an alien, as you call me, but neither I nor any of my comrades want to take over your planet. We are merely advisors, trying to right some of the wrongs that have been done here over the centuries."

"Ms. Lewis-Phillips wants me to stay here to be educated. I don't know what to do. You aren't going to use me for medical research, are you? That's what Patrick says you do here."

"Patrick is mistaken. We don't do that kind of research here or at any of our other bases. Our research is done to perfect vaccines and medications to heal the illnesses of all the humans on this planet. I'm confused, you're very well spoken, but you mentioned education."

Once again, Christopher related the story of his birth and upbringing at Henderson Ranch. Like Caroline, Hodia was moved to tears.

"I never thought I would hear of such a horror story in this day and age. I studied some of the histories of the orphanages, work houses and the like in the eighteenth and nineteenth centuries, but I never thought I would hear about such things in modern times. This will have to be investigated and those responsible will be dealt with. I agree with Caroline, I would be honored to have you come to live at the complex and allow us to see to your education. From what I can tell, you have a fine mind. Perhaps you can become a link between us and the militants. The way I see it, education and knowledge of the past are going to be very important in the future of Earth."

Caroline wondered if Christopher could feel the love radiating from Hodia's words. Seeing this angry young man crying like a frightened child, made her want to pull him into her arms and give him the comfort she was certain he'd never enjoyed at any time in his life.

"I-I would like to have an education. Can I see Patrick and tell him of these plans before he leaves?"

Hodia nodded and held out her hand. Caroline was pleased when Christopher took it without hesitation.

Outside the door, the security guard waited for them to exit the room. Hodia dismissed him with nothing more than a wave of her hand and the three of them made their way back to the conference room.

~ * ~

Aaron worried when Caroline agreed to meet privately with the young militant. Even with a security guard going with them, once they were in the private office, anything could happen.

"Why did Christopher want to talk to that bitch alone?" Patrick spat out, his words laced with anger.

"I have no idea but you will not use such vulgar language in reference to my wife. I'd like for you to answer a question for me."

"Why should I, old man?"

"Because this man has done nothing to harm you," Dr. Gratan responded. "To be truthful, no one here has done you harm. We are all interested in a peaceful end to this protest. What is it that has made you so angry?"

Patrick hesitated for a moment, as though considering his answer. "All this talk about history is ridiculous. I went to school and I never heard anything about what that lady was saying. I have no idea who this Adolph Hitler was and I don't need to know. Our group is as old as time itself.

My parents taught me about the inferiority of all the races but our own. Now you want to bring up ancient history and it makes no sense."

"Your education, like that of most of Earth's population, is lacking when it comes to the history Ms. Lewis-Phillips has brought to light," President Addison said. "I have done a lot of research into the history of this country and I admit I knew next to nothing about these things. I'm willing to learn from the mistakes of the past. Would you be willing to call off this protest and weigh all of your options?"

Before Patrick could answer, the door to the conference room opened. Aaron was surprised to see Caroline, Christopher and Hodia enter the room.

Patrick looked up at his friend. From the expression on his face, it was evident he could see something had changed as far as Christopher was concerned.

"I was afraid you wouldn't come back, buddy," Patrick said, grasping Christopher's forearm. "What did they do to you?"

"They didn't do anything. They offered to give me the education I was denied and the chance to learn about my heritage. You've been good to me, but I think I want more out of life. What you don't know is that my DNA says I have Native American blood. With that, I can't be a member of your group. I should have told you this in the beginning, but I had no idea what it meant."

The wind seemed to go out of Patrick's sails. "Do you mean to tell me there might be something to this history crap?"

"There is," President Addison replied. "Since you're the leader of these people, would you agree to work with us, and by us, I mean, everyone in this complex as well as the military and myself, to bring this to a peaceful end?"

The room became suddenly silent. Everyone looked to Patrick, anxious to know what his answer would be.

"Will we be under arrest?"

"I give you my word, if you will work with us, there will be no charges brought against any of you. The one condition is that you must turn in your weapons. Is that something you can agree to?"

Slowly, Patrick nodded his head in agreement. "I'm man enough to take you at your word. Maybe this history thing might be good for our country."

He turned toward Christopher. "Are you sure you want to stay here, man?"

"I'm sure. You've been good to me, but I need to know who I am. It's possible I have people like me who will accept me. These people aren't our enemies. They want to help all of the people of Earth. I'm not the smartest person in our group, but I want to learn everything I've been denied in the past."

Again, Patrick grasped Christopher's forearm. "You're a good man. If you think this is a good move, I tend to agree with you. President Addison has said there will be no charges brought against any of us. It's entirely possible, the time for protests and war is over."

Aaron breathed a sigh of relief and turned his attention to Caroline. From the expression on her face, he knew she played a major part in the decision Christopher made, just as President Addison did with Patrick.

Chapter Twenty-Two

"What happened with Christopher?" Aaron asked, once they were back at their condo.

"I've never heard such a sad story in my entire life. His parents were headed toward the hospital because his mother was having complications with her pregnancy when they were in a hover craft accident. His father died at the scene and his mother lived long enough to give birth to him before she also died. He was premature and not expected to live. Because of the DNA done at birth, it was discovered he had Native American heritage, making him ineligible for adoption. Therefore, he was placed at a boy's ranch where he was denied a formal education."

"How could that happen in this day and age?"

"We're not sure, but Hodia was so outraged, she vowed to find out where this ranch was and to have them shut down. It's inhumane to deny a child an education because of his heritage. Hopefully, once we see to his education, we can look into finding relatives who were never advised of his birth twenty years ago."

Caroline yawned broadly, alerting Aaron to just how exhausted she was.

"This has been a trying few days for both of us," he said. "Why don't we go to bed? I can see you're exhausted and I know I am as well. Tomorrow will be another full day. If I know you, I'm certain you will want to begin Christopher's education."

"That was my intent as well, but Hodia has other ideas. She's already making arrangements for his housing as well as some of the best tutors the complex has to offer. I'll be working with him in his history studies, but I will have to take things easy."

Aaron noticed the slight smile that crossed Caroline's lips. "Is there something you aren't telling me?"

Caroline's smile broadened as she put her hand to his cheek. "Do you think we're too old to become parents? I hope we aren't, because in about seven months our child will be born. I don't know how this could have happened because of the suspended animation, but I think God has great plans for this new life we have created."

Aaron pulled her into an embrace. "I knew marrying you was the best thing I could have done with my life. Something also tells me not only are we going to have a baby to love but Christopher will become very important in our lives. I'm so blessed to have met you. From now on, there will never be a dull moment in either of our lives."

About the Author

At the age of fifteen, Sherry Derr-Wille walked into her sophomore English class and fell in love with writing. Her teacher, Earl, Brockman, "The Duke of Earl," announced that anyone getting an A on the first test could sit in the back of the room and write for a year. Since no one told her to stop, she continued to write for over forty years before becoming published in 2003.

Married to her high school sweetheart, Bob, for over fifty years, she calls him a saint for putting up with a crazy writer. In other words, "You don't have to be crazy to write a book, but you're certifiable when you write over eighty of them." Together they raised three children, have nine grandchildren and five great granddaughters.

Born a country girl, she loves living in a mid-sized city close to the Illinois border with Wisconsin. Being retired gives her time to follow her heart writing, along with editing for several private clients and Rogue Phoenix Press.

Coming May 2021 by the Author

at

Rogue Phoenix Press

Unwanted in a New World
The New World Book Two

Chapter One

Spring 2100

Juanita Little Horse, wiped away her tears as she and her boyfriend, Carter Jennings, took the last of her possessions out of her parents' house. Carter was white and although she knew her parents each had whites in their background, they had forbidden her to be with him.

When she could hide the evidence of her pregnancy no longer, she broke the news to her parents. Their immediate response was that she was no longer welcome in their home.

"You were taught better than to give into the demands of the first man to pay you any attention," her father accused. "You are no longer a daughter of mine. If this man is so important to you, he can have you."

She'd turned to her mother for support only to be met with a cold, hard stare.

"Fine," she shouted as she started packing her belongings. "This is you grandchild, but you will never see him. We're going far away from here."

Carter helped her load the last of her belongings into the cargo area of the hover craft. Once everything was secured, they took their seats and prepared for lift off.

Sadly, she looked back at the only home she'd ever known. She thought perhaps her parents would at least wave good-bye to her, but she was mistaken. The front yard of their neat home was empty. Even her younger brother and sister were conveniently out of sight.

"Don't cry, honey. We can crash at my place until we know where we want to settle. It's not as big as your parents' house, but it's in a good neighborhood. I have a lead on a job in Colorado. They said they'd let me know by the end of the week and we can say good-bye to Montana forever. It will be the two of us against the world."

"What about your parents?"

"I told you, they are no longer with us."

Juanita's tears flowed faster. "It must be the pregnancy. I'm usually not someone to cry at the drop of a hat."

She paused and suddenly remembered something. "I-I don't have my identification. I was in such a hurry. I didn't have time to look for my birth certificate. I have no way to prove who I am. We have to go back and get it."

"Do you know how far we've come? If we turn back now, we won't get to my apartment in Sundance until well after dark. This is an old enough model craft that the night vision doesn't work for shit."

Panicked, Juana reached for the controls, sending the hover craft into a tailspin.

~ * ~

Sirens screamed through the night as emergency craft converged on the Laughlin Ranch, located at the southeast corner of the state of Montana.

"I saw it go down," Pete Laughlin said. "It looked like the pilot lost control and it went into a spin before it crashed, right here in the middle of my cow pasture. From what I could tell, there were only two people in it."

"It looks like the man is dead, but he's so badly burned, I don't know if anyone could identify him, Sheriff," the first medical tech on the scene reported. "I don't know how it happened, but the girl was thrown away from the fire. She's still alive, but probably not for long. She's also pregnant. If we want to save the baby, we'll have to transport her to the closest hospital as soon as possible."

The captain in charge agreed and watched as the rescuers secured her into the ambulance. He would have wanted to go with her and see if she could give him some sort of a statement as to how the accident occurred. Instead he knew he needed to stay behind and try to figure out who these people were.

Debris was spread across the lush, green pasture. Checking it out, he decided one of both of them were in the process of moving to a different location.

"Who are you?" Sheriff Collins asked, knowing full well he wouldn't receive an answer.

Turning to one of the officers with him he asked, "Were you able to get a VIN on the craft?"

"Everything was burned too badly. How the girl survived is anyone's guess. If you ask me, I'd say this was a solen vehicle, but who would steal something this old? The damn thing shouldn't have been flying in the first place."

"From the looks of things, they were just kids. The girl couldn't have been anywhere near her twentieth birthday. It's a shame, a damn dirty shame."

~ * ~

The emergency room of the country hospital buzzed with activity. Dr. Christopher Parker got the call about a hover craft accident on a remote ranch several miles away from the hospital. He wasn't looking forward to receiving the sole survivor of the crash. From the report he'd received, his patient was a young woman who was at least seven months pregnant. The prognosis didn't sound good. It was entirely possible he would lose two patients before the night was over.

The air ambulance arrived and two med techs wheeled in a young woman lying motionless on the gurney.

Dr. Parker wasted no time in examining his patient. Although her skin color was fair, he could see her blood matted hair was originally dark black and her high cheek bones denoted a Native American heritage in her lineage.

It was evident she wouldn't last the night, but there was a fetal heartbeat. He knew he had to do his best to save this tiny life. Calling up to the operating room, he made arrangements for the Cererian section to be done so the child could be delivered.

An hour later he received word the child had been born, but the mother perished. Being so premature, the baby boy weighed only one pound eleven and a half ounces. It was entirely possible he wouldn't survive until the next morning.

"Do you know the name of the mother?" the nurse who approached him asked.

"From what the police have told me, neither the boy nor the girl had any identification. I know we have to name him something. I'll give him my first name and since the accident happened on the Laughlin Ranch, why don't we name him Christopher Laughlin? It won't matter because I'm certain the boy won't make it through tonight to say nothing of growing to adulthood."

~ * ~

Six months later, Dr. Parker was surprised when he received a call from the neonatal unit saying Christopher was ready to be released from the hospital. It took him a minute to recall who they were talking about.

The vision of the dying young mother and the premature baby who didn't have a snowball's chance in hell of surviving came to mind.

"Who are you going to release him to?" he finally asked.

"Since he has no parents and we know of no other family, we're sending him to Henderson Ranch in Nevada. They take in unadoptable children."

Dr. Parker was confused. "Why is he unadoptable?"

"Don't you know? No agencies want to deal in mixed breed children. His DNA came back and his origins are Cheyenne and European. The Cheyenne don't want him and there's not a couple listed in the system who want to take on someone like him. With his mother being Native American and his father completely unknown, it's a risk to say the very least. It was the thought of the officers at the scene that the hover craft the parents were flying in when the crash happened was stolen. Of course, with the Vin number burned off, there was no way to verify their assumptions. Would you want to adopt a child with that kind of a background? Henderson Ranch is the best place for him."

Dr. Parker tended to agree with the nurse, but he felt sorry or the child who would grow up without the love of his parents. At this point in his life, he wasn't able to even think of adopting a child. He and his wife had three children. Between his busy schedule at the hospital and her position at a prestigious accounting firm, there was no time to take on what could turn out to become a very troubled child. It was for the best if he was sent somewhere equipped to handle such children.

Also by the Author
at
Rogue Phoenix Press

My Uncle the King
The Aliens Book Two

When three contingencies took off from their dying planet, Plantas, only two arrived at their destination unharmed. When the lost contingency is hit with a meteor storm, only one ship survives and makes it to their destination of Nalo. Over the generations, the descendants of the original refugees become the ruling class of their adopted planet. Even the rebel group, the Pure Of Nalo, are unable to unseat the monarchy. When relations with Earth are established, it is Prince Nicos who leaves Nalo to find love on an alien planet and bring back new ideas as well as his Earthly family to save the throne and the people of Nalo.

Prologue

My story begins many years ago when my father, Prince Nicos of Nalo, had a falling out with his twin brother, Prince Miro. Even in the womb they had been bitter enemies, each trying to get the most nourishment and fighting to be the first to be brought into the world by their mother, Queen Liona.

Miro, being the first born, was the heir to the throne. With this knowledge, he lorded his superiority over his two-minutes' younger brother throughout the time they were growing up.

Nicos, although not the heir apparent, soon learned to ignore his older brother and dedicate his life to education as well as military service.

While away on a diplomatic mission to Earth to become Nalo's Ambassador to Earth, he met my mother and fell in love.

Of course, I'm way ahead of my story, so I will let you read that which came before, so you can better understand my background.

Chapter One

Grato prepared to leave his home planet, Plantas. In a matter of days, Plantas would be destroyed and all of the old and infirm people who were staying behind would be no more.

Over the past few weeks, everyone had been planning for this journey. In the distant past, his people had gone to the planet Nalo to help the ancient people settle the land. In addition, they taught the same people to use written language, medicine and mathematics. Likewise, his best friend Ragnar's family went to Seros. Therefore, these were the worlds to which they would return.

Grato and his family were going to be on the first ship to lift off from Plantas while the woman he loved, Tarena, would be in the last ship. He hated the thought of being separated from her for the duration of the journey, but they were going to be mated once they both landed safely. With that knowledge, he decided he could stand the separation.

A week earlier, his family left to go to the first launch site on the other side of the planet. He protested going with his parents because it meant being separated from Tarena for longer than necessary, but it was important for his father, as for his family, to be on the first ship.

He settled into his seat and prepared for lift-off. As their ship soared into the air, he was able to watch the other ships destined for Nalo do likewise. They flew in a perfect formation for several months.

As an engineering expert, he spent many hours every day on the bridge. During those long hours, he was often in contact with the other ships, including the one carrying Tarena and her family.

The first medical officer, Wasla, made a daily trip to the bridge to not only check on those who were flying the ship but also to contact her soon-to-be-mate, Paren, who was on the third ship in the formation.

"Have you been in contact with Tarena today, Grato?" Wasla asked, when she approached him.

"Yes. Everything on their ship is going well. With luck we should reach Nalo without any difficulty within the next month."

"I'll be happy to be on solid land again. Many of our people have developed Time Warp Fever. I pray they will all be well by the time we land."

Grato agreed. He'd heard about the spread of Time Warp Fever and was even starting to feel some of the symptoms of it. He'd experienced a problem with vertigo and developed a nagging headache, but said nothing.

Wasla went about her daily routine, checking everyone on the bridge. By the time she got to Grato, she had a worried expression on her face.

"You don't look so well, my friend. Let me take your temperature."

As much as Grato protested, she soon used her wand thermometer to check his temperature. "I'm afraid I must send you to the sick bay. Your temperature is elevated and I can tell by looking at you, you are experiencing some of the symptoms of Time Warp Fever."

"That's nonsense. You know I'm one of the healthiest people on this ship. I have duties to perform. I don't have time for something like this."

"You do have time for it, son," his father interrupted. "I've noticed several signs of the disease making their presence known in you. It's best if you do as Wasla says. She's our top medical officer."

Reluctantly, Grato gave up his place at the helm of the ship and followed Wasla to the area designated as the sick bay. Even walking those few steps was difficult for him as his balance was now completely off. He was surprised at how much he had to depend on Wasla to support his weight as he made his way through the ship.

Passing through the other populated areas of the craft, he saw the worried expressions on the faces of his friends and family.

Is it possible I show more of the symptoms of this debilitating disease than I first thought?

Once at the sick bay, two nurses insisted on helping him out of his clothes and into a gown. He hated having to disrobe in front of these women, but knew it was necessary. When the fever broke, he was told, he would break out into a sweat and he certainly didn't want to ruin his robes.

The IV had been successfully inserted into his body when the ship began to shudder. IV poles toppled over, people were thrown from their beds, and medical personnel hung onto whatever they could to avoid falling to the floor.

"What was that?"

The question resonated throughout the ship without an answer for many minutes. They remained in an eerie silence until at last the shaking stopped and people were able to return to their seats or beds.

After what seemed like endless hours, Grato's father left the bridge and walked through the ship.

"We have been hit by a meteor shower. I was able to watch what was happening. I am afraid ours is the only ship to have survived. We will be able to make it to Nalo, but our communications with our sister ships as well as the missions to Seros and Earth have been completely destroyed. We will be traveling under diminished power so the remainder of the trip will take longer than anticipated. That being the case, we will also be rationing our food supplies."

Grato didn't know much about medicine but he did know patients suffering from Time Warp Fever needed added nourishment. He thought about his ability to heal. He was in the early stages of the disease and could probably survive until they reached Nalo, but what about the others in their party, who were in more advanced stages?

Once he finally evaluated their status, he thought of the other ships in their fleet. How could they all be lost? Was it even possible Tarena and Paren were dead, taken away from them in the blink of an eye?

Beside him Wasla grieved for the loss of her promised life mate. Shedding tears seemed too unmanly for him, but he couldn't stop the flow of them at the thought of his loss. Tarena was to have been his mate. Now he knew how his friend Ragnar felt when he'd been told Nina was going to Earth while he would be sent to Seros.

Even with the short rations, they managed to reach Nalo only a few days later than they expected. It took several days and a lot of work for the communications officers to be able to communicate with the inhabitants of the planet. It was amazing how advanced these people were. They were able to send out a tractor beam to bring their craft safely to a predestined landing area. Once they safely landed, they were greeted by members of the medical and scientific contingency.

At Wasla's insistence, the medical community of Nalo was told of the Time Warp Fever that affected many of their population.

Grato looked forward to being one of the first of their kind to contact the people with whom they would be living and working, but that was not to be. Instead of meeting with the leaders, medical personnel entered the ship and brought with them stretchers in order to transport those who had Time Warp Fever to waiting air ambulances for transportation to hospitals.

He began to protest but as soon as he left the ship, his father was at his side. "Go with them, son. We have informed them of what you are experiencing, and they are equipped to bring you back to good health."

"Your father is right," Wasla agreed. "I will be going with you and conferring with their healers. You will see, the future for us will be a bright one. Once you are past this illness…"

He knew she left the remainder of what she was saying unsaid. *Our lives were going to be here on Nalo but the lives of our loved ones are gone forever.* He would never be mated with Tarena just as Wasla and Paren would not be together again.

The next few days passed in a blur. At the hospital, he was able to see the broadcasts of the arrival of his people on Nalo. Thankfully, they had been accepted and had begun assimilating themselves into Nalo's society.

It was days later before he was finally well enough to leave the hospital and reunite with the other survivors of his party. While in the hospital, Wasla hadn't left his side. As much as they both grieved the loss of the ones they loved, he knew a relationship was beginning to form.

The Return of the Ancients
The Aliens Book One

Nina is devastated when she realizes she must leave Plantas along with the man who is to become her mate, Ragnar, and her best friend, Tarena. When Nina arrives on Earth in Peru at the Nazca plains, she is greeted by a young archaeology student, Rand Jacobson. Even though she is attracted to Rand, she is still grieving the loss of Ragnar.

Ragnar is surprised when, after being greeted as a god on the planet Seros, the military opens fire on his family. After being taken prisoner, he is treated like a lab rat until a scientist, Geni, comes to his rescue. At her estate, he learns the physicians who work with her have saved the lives of his family and friends.

You Again

While attending college at the University of Wisconsin in the 1960s, Carole Martinson fell in love and eloped with Phillip Vanderlin. When his parents realized she was a farmer's daughter and below them socially, they insisted they divorce.

Fast forward to 2019 and Carole is invited to a wedding cruise financed by her granddaughter's fiancé's grandfather. With no knowledge about the groom's family, Carole flies to Florida for the cruise she and her second husband never got to take. Upon her arrival, she immediately recognizes Phillip.

Phillip never forgot his first love. He is thrilled when he realizes the grandmother is the girl he was forced to leave behind so many years ago.

www.ingramcontent.com/pod-product-compliance
Lightning Source LLC
Chambersburg PA
CBHW051958220626
47052CB00004B/994